PRAI

The Last Party

"Even savvy veterans who predict every twist will keep turning the pages compulsively as the mystery curdles into suspense."

—*Kirkus Reviews*

A Fatal Affair

"Nothing is remotely routine in Torre's heady brew of serial murder spiced with fraud, torture, impersonation, and assorted celebrity hijinks . . . you won't put it down till every last drop of blood has been shed."

—*Kirkus Reviews*

"A thriller with surprises aplenty and a breezy pace that includes well-written characters and the singular challenge of looking for truth 'in a sea of professional liars and seducers,' this novel is sure to have wide appeal."

—*Library Journal*

A Familiar Stranger

"A whiplash suspenser that's a model of its kind."

—*Kirkus Reviews*

"The author skillfully reveals the characters' many lies and secrets. Torre knows how to keep the reader guessing."

—*Publishers Weekly*

The Good Lie

"Ambitious and twisty . . . Great bedtime reading for insomniacs and people willing to act like insomniacs just this once."

—*Kirkus Reviews*

"This kinky tale is compulsively readable."

—*Publishers Weekly*

"A blend of serial-killer story, court cases, and even romance, this is a tricky story that will keep readers going."

—*Parkersburg News and Sentinel*

Every Last Secret

"Deliciously, sublimely nasty: *Mean Girls* for grown-ups."

—*Kirkus Reviews*

"Torre keeps the suspense high . . . Readers will be riveted from page one."

—*Publishers Weekly*

"A glamorous and seductive novel that will suck you in and knock you sideways. I love this story, these characters, and the raw emotion they generated in me. I devoured every word. Exceptional."

—Tarryn Fisher, *New York Times* bestselling author

"Raw and riveting. A clever ride that will make you question everyone and everything."

—Meredith Wild, #1 *New York Times* bestselling author

A
HAPPY
MARRIAGE

OTHER TITLES BY A. R. TORRE

A

HAPPY

MARRIAGE

A. R. TORRE

Published by Thomas & Mercer, Seattle

www.apub.com

Amazon, the Amazon logo, and Thomas & Mercer are trademarks of Amazon.com, Inc., or its affiliates.

EU product safety contact:
Amazon Media EU S. à r.l.
38, avenue John F. Kennedy, L-1855 Luxembourg
amazonpublishing-gpsr@amazon.com

ISBN-13: 9781662519598 (paperback)
ISBN-13: 9781662519604 (digital)

Cover design by Jarrod Taylor
Cover image: © Ruben Mario Ramos / ArcAngel; © Bulgac / Getty; © natrot / Shutterstock

Printed in the United States of America

To my husband, who makes it easy to write a woman who is madly in love.

CHAPTER 1

JOE

I watch my wife eat her cereal and think about the first girl I killed. She ate cereal in a very different manner, setting down her spoon in between bites and waiting as she chewed, her jaw moving in a lazy and circular fashion as she ground the sugary flakes into mush, then swallowing and pausing a beat, as if to see if it would stay down. Then she'd pick up the spoon and start the process again.

My wife shovels a new bite in while the first is mid-chew. She hunches over the bowl, her gaze pinned to my face as she listens to me talk. The Cheerios are an afterthought, her spoon passing between the bowl and her full lips without pause. Chew, slurp, brush a tendril of hair out of her face, plunge the spoon into the bowl, lick her lips, open, and gulp another spoonful.

It's a masterful coordination, made more beautiful because she is oblivious that it is happening. All her attention is glued on me, and I know that just as I am noticing every detail, so is she. She focuses on the press of my lips together when I pause, the raise of my brows when I ask a question, the moment I reach up and straighten the knot of my tie.

The first dead girl, she didn't listen to me. She didn't notice anything. She was too focused on herself, on her clothing, her goals, her music, her money, her grades. Her mind was running a race just to keep up with herself. When I killed her, she was probably thinking of the funeral and reaction more than the pain.

What would they bury her in?

Who would cry?

What would the obituary say?

They never found her body, so the burial outfit never mattered. There was also no obituary, but to her credit, there were a lot of tears shed.

If I ever kill my wife, I'll make sure they find her body.

She deserves that.

She deserves everything.

CHAPTER 2

It takes almost two days for anyone to notice that Reese Bishop is dead. It's the flies that cause the discovery. On Saturday morning, they buzz against the window of the kitchen, a dozen small notification systems of fragile wings and oily legs, their mouths masticating bits of Reese's flesh as they batter against the panes. The taps of their bodies against the glass catch the attention of the mailman, who pauses in his attempt to wedge the furniture catalog into the mail container beside the front door.

Brad Thomas hitches the heavy messenger bag up on his shoulder and hesitates at the sight of the insects' movements. Reese Bishop didn't complete a request to hold her mail, and it was odd for her box to be full. Two odds, as his wife likes to say, don't make a right.

His gaze drops to the thick catalog, which now sticks halfway out of the box. Leaving it in place, he sidesteps over to the window, cups a hand over his right eye, and leans forward to look through the dirty glass.

The fifty-two-year-old woman is sitting at the small round table in the kitchen, her head down on the red tablecloth. Her hair is pulled back with a fluffy scrunchie, and she has a small flower tattooed just behind her ear. Her face is turned toward him, her eyes dark, her mouth hanging open.

Flies crawl across her pale white skin and into and out of her mouth. Below her eyebrows are two dark balls of movement, and the postman inhales sharply at the realization that the flies are feasting on her eyes.

CHAPTER 3

DINAH

I rinse out my cereal bowl and place it in the rack beside the sink. Joe's plate is there, the fork from his eggs sticking out of the silverware cup. It gives me such a sense of domestic bliss to follow his act each morning, both of us doing our part to keep our house in order, to respect each other's time and space. Other couples leave their dishes out, expecting the spouse to be their maid, but Joe and I have never done that.

I'm pouring coffee into a thermos when my phone buzzes. I check the display and answer it, attempting to hold it in the crook of my neck as I stack and tear open three Splenda packets. "Marino." The phone slips and I grab it just before it hits the counter.

"Dinah, this is Lieutenant Paul Franks. I was told you're covering homicide for Rita Perez?"

"Yep. What's going on?" I smile at Joe as he walks by. He pauses and presses a kiss to the back of my head.

"We have a possible victim in Montebello. Address is 23 Luther Drive. There's a couple of uniforms there now; medical and scene techs are on the way."

I empty the packets into the thermos and motion to the fridge. My husband is already opening the door, withdrawing the half gallon of milk and passing it to me. "23 Luther Drive. Got it. I'll head that way now."

Joe's gaze meets mine, and I don't have to explain what the call is about.

In our marriage, death is a common disruption of our peace.

CHAPTER 4

DINAH

It takes twenty-four minutes to get to Montebello from our home in the Hollywood Hills. On the way, I'm honked at a half-dozen times, flipped off, cut off, and approached by panhandlers. In other words, a typical Tuesday-morning commute in Los Angeles.

Normally, I'd be headed into Beverly Hills, where the crime is heavily dissected between the uber rich and the poor, the tax base of the former helping us handle the disturbances of the latter. Montebello is a different story, with thin resources and an understaffed department. I'm not looking forward to meeting and working with a new crew, but that is what you do when one homicide detective out of twenty in a city like Los Angeles is on leave. You cover. You help out. If I'm ever out of commission or on extended leave, someone will take my beat, research my murders, and make my arrests.

I despise the thought and spend nights lying awake in bed and thinking of someone like Robertson miscategorizing evidence and overlooking clues.

Is it wrong to want all the murders to myself?

I pull down Luther and appear to be the last one to the scene. The scene techs, coroner, and some black-and-whites have sucked up all the available spots on the residential street that is solidly lower middle class.

I snag a spot a block down, between a Nissan coupe and a minivan. My old partner would have griped at how far I'm parked from the curb, but Oley isn't here anymore, so I leave it alone and step out, sending a quick apology up to him.

I don't miss the guy; the job is much easier solo. That being said, there are moments when I turn to say something to Oley at a crime scene or in the middle of an interview and he isn't there. He isn't there smacking a big wad of bubblegum, his pen drumming against the inside of his thigh, the buttons on the front of his dress shirt straining against his wide chest, his goofy smile stretched across his sunburned face. I was annoyed by him until he was gone, and now I wonder if, besides Joe and my first crush, he's the only man I ever loved.

Oley would have described today's weather as being hot enough to scald a lizard. He loved that phrase and always guffawed after it, as if he'd said the wittiest thing. I fan myself with my neck badge as I cross the street. The skirt suit, which had seemed perfect inside our air-conditioned house, is a mistake. My pantyhose are already slipping down my left thigh, and I can feel my underarms collecting sweat. I quicken my steps and promise myself that I'll lose the jacket as soon as I step inside. A fly buzzes in front of me, and I swipe it away and smile at a uniform who passes by, his face bored, the gesture not returned. Fucking Montebello.

I step over the curb and up on the sidewalk and watch as another unmarked car pulls up to the front of the house and attempts to take the space at the end of the driveway. I squint, trying to see who is behind the wheel.

The car's tire scrapes the edge of the curb, and the faint thump of music comes from its interior. The sedan settles into place, and the engine shuts down as the door opens. A man who looks like he could be a basketball player unfolds from the car, all dark and messy hair, an olive complexion, and a suit as stifling hot as mine. As he tucks a corn-flower-blue tie against his dress shirt and strides up the drive toward me, I immediately note all the things wrong with this picture.

Age: too young.

Attractiveness: too much.

Attitude: too confident.

I know every detective in this town, but he's not familiar to me. I frown as he approaches, trying to understand who he is and why he's here.

"You must be Dinah Marino." He smiles big as his long strides eat up the space between us. "I'm Freddie Hodgkins." He sticks out his hand and I take it.

Freddie Hodgkins. The name doesn't ring a bell.

"What department?" I ask, pushing my sunglasses up on my head so I can see him better.

"I'm currently patrol but in the training program for detective. I'm shadowing Ron Memphis this month."

I smile, though the thought of Ron makes me want to vomit. I still have the imprint of his stare on my ass from the last all-district meeting.

"Well, I'm covering for Rita Perez," I say crisply as a bead of sweat runs down the back of my neck. "Ron's not on Montebello."

"He's actually in the hospital." He grimaces. "Really bad case of gout. So they have me shadowing other detectives. Sent me over here when this call came in."

Screw that. The last thing I need is a trainee stuck to my side, questioning every move I make.

"Sorry that you're stuck with me on this one." He shrugs and smiles, and that lethal combination has probably unlocked every door in his handsome little life, but it doesn't do anything for me. Instead, the idea of a trainee—especially an attractive one—digging through my scene sends bile rising to my throat.

I glance toward the home's front door, anxious to get inside. "Okay," I say, trying to think of a reason, any reason, to get him back in his car and out of my hair.

Nothing comes to me, so I head up a skinny sidewalk that cuts through a faded-green artificial turf lawn toward the front porch. He follows closely, his dress shoes crunching, and now I won't be able to take off my jacket, not without wondering if the white blouse I'm wearing is clinging to my breasts. For the second time since leaving the car, I curse my outfit. Joe hates when I wear this shirt; he thinks it's inappropriate for work, and maybe he's right. My husband rarely has an opinion on my attire. I should have listened to him this morning.

There's a kit by the front door mat, and I dip down and grab a set of booties and latex gloves. After pulling the stretchy plastic over my flats, I work on the gloves and watch as he does the same.

"I'll dictate if you take notes. You got a notepad?" I ask.

He reaches into his jacket's interior pocket and pulls out a small red spiral-bound and a pen.

I grab the front doorknob and consider him for a moment. "I'm not used to having someone shadowing me, so please forgive me if I am a little . . ." I pause, trying to find the right word. "Grouchy, at times."

He smiles wide, as if I've said something funny. "I'll grow on you," he reassures me, grabbing the door's edge and pulling it all the way open.

Yeah. That will be Joe's concern.

CHAPTER 5

DINAH

Freddie smells like a vanilla-and-coconut bath scrub I used in my twenties. The scent keeps floating over to me whenever he moves, and it clashes with the putrid and slightly fruity smell of a dead body. I use both hands to pull the elastic bands of a face mask behind my ears, covering my nose and mouth. There. Let his distracting scent try to permeate that.

I check the lock on the wide kitchen window and do the same for the back door. Neither look disturbed, and I verbalize the observation, then crouch beside a scuffed-up round dining table and stare at Reese Bishop's slack expression, a small pool of dried vomit beneath her chin. "What made you suspect foul play?" I glance at the medical examiner, who chugs a bottle of water by the back door. I know this woman, and of all the MEs, I'm glad it's Monica. We've worked at least a dozen scenes together, and she's a good mix of attentive and adaptive.

"There's an empty pentobarbital bottle in the trash. I'll verify it with the autopsy and blood work, but the most likely cause of death is overdose. I'll leave it up to you if it's self-inflicted or foul play. That's why you get the big bucks."

I chuckle, well aware that Monica probably outearns me by a factor of four. "Okay. I'll be quick so you can take the body."

"No problem." She crumples the water bottle and I glance at Freddie, who has his little notepad out, pen at the ready, a page of notes already down.

I focus on the scene in front of me. No reason I wouldn't be able to knock out this report in a couple of hours and make it back to my part of town for lunch.

I clear my throat and begin. "Female seated at a round table just off the kitchen. Looks like she was eating breakfast and passed out. She looks to be late forties. Dark shoulder-length hair with gray roots. No wedding ring. Pale complexion." I tilt my head, spotting something under the stretched-out collar of the T-shirt she's wearing. The edge of something fabric. A Band-Aid or . . . I use the tip of my pen to pull the neckline to one side, revealing the curve of a collarbone and . . . there. "A port." I look up at Freddie, who is standing beside me, his crotch at eye level. "I'll pull her medical history, find out if this is for cancer or something else."

"I'm a step ahead of you," Monica says. "Advanced heart disease, was denied a transplant because she's a smoker. It was terminal, according to her doc. I ordered her full history, which I'll put in the file as soon as I get it."

"Okay, so likely suicide." I straighten to standing.

Freddie frowns; of course he doesn't like the suicide angle. Newbies love dramatic, complicated murders, but he's going to be disappointed. I'm three minutes into this scene and already know the evidence won't point to murder. No forced entry, no sign of a struggle. Easy peasy.

I do a slow visual sweep of the cramped room. Faded-blue wallpaper with a pattern of chickens. The milk in the cereal bowl is congealed, the sour smell adding to the scent cocktail of Freddie's cologne and the decomposing body. A cup of black coffee. A newspaper, open to a word search game, half-completed. I'm not sure if that's a clue toward suicide or murder. If I planned to die, would I want to spend my last hour staring at a puzzle?

It's a question for Joe—not that I'll discuss this with him. Separation of church and state, and all that. I handle my business, he handles his.

"So, no note," Freddie pipes in.

"Doesn't look like it." I turn slowly, double-checking every surface. Freddie writes something down, and I envision how tonight's dinner conversation with Joe will go.

"Did he flirt with you?" No.

"Not even a little?" No.

He won't believe me, will want to meet Freddie, to do that male dance of handshakes and eye contact and dick-measuring; then there will be a whole new round of questions for me, at a time when it should be over.

Joe has a lot of strengths, but trust isn't one of them. His suspicion is a two-way highway between us, paved in love and fortified with rebars of verification, which is why I probably won't tell him about Freddie at all.

I turn from the body. "Let's tour the house."

The crime scene techs move away, like opposing magnets, wherever we go. It's funny, even though this is a different crew from the one we use in Beverly Hills, there is that familiar hostility present, which I never understand. It feels like a competition of who can find out what without the other team knowing. It shouldn't be like that, especially not in an industry where lives are at stake. I mentioned it once to one of the other shields, and they looked at me as if I was crazy, like they had no idea what I was talking about. So maybe it's just something about me the CSIs don't like.

Either way, when Freddie and I go into the primary bedroom, they leave it and provide no information as to what they've photographed or whether anything in the room contributes to the scene.

The room is drenched in floral print, a variety of designs covering the walls, the curtains, the bedspread, and the pillows. It smells vaguely of cat, but I don't see one anywhere, and there's been no damage to the body. That's the telltale sign of cats: they start eating almost immediately, which tells me all I need to know about having one as a pet. Dogs will starve to death beside their owners. Not cats. They start munching the ears first.

There's something that always throws me off about being in a dead woman's room. The weight of it—not of the death, but of everything involved in the aftermath. Someone will need to go through each of these drawers. Her trash can. That dirty pair of underwear or the dusty vibrator in the bedside drawer. Her knickknacks on the dresser. The earrings pushed into the corkboard on the wall.

It's why it takes me an extra half hour before I ever leave the house for weekends at the ranch. What if we died while away? I couldn't have my colleagues walking through my house, opening drawers and digging through our trash. I've worked too hard to make our home a sanctuary of peace and order, each item carefully curated with a goal of cohesion.

In comparison, Reese's selections are much more utilitarian. Price over beauty. Function over form. She has a giant blue body pillow that is stained and ripped in one corner. An annual calendar with pigs in various costumes hangs from a nail on the yellow wall. October 25 has a heart around it, and I stare at it for a long moment.

October is a bad month, in general. The month I almost lost everything. The month my younger sister got married. The month serial killers Gary Evans and Mack Ray Edwards were born, among others. No wonder the holiday of horror falls inside it.

We spend almost an hour in the ten-foot-by-ten-foot space. I search under her mattress and through her jewelry box. I look in all the places where secrets are kept but don't find any.

"No computer," Freddie remarks. "Have you seen a phone anywhere?"

"No."

"Suicide victims don't hide their phones."

An astute observation for a newbie.

"Agreed." I let out a breath and think through it. The lack of a phone is something a DA would pounce on, if this case ever crosses their desk. But the missing phone is also like a body. Without one, it's hard to prove murder, even though the absence points to it.

I stand. "Let's look at the rest of the house."

The second bedroom raises a bigger question. It's a young woman's room, one that smells of fruity body sprays. Everything is neat and stylish, the color scheme all creams and pinks, the bed made with a fuzzy set of pillows that spelled out J-E-B. The closet is in perfect order, with even rows of dark jeans, teeny tops, and at least a dozen pairs of shoes. I thumb through a stack of matching folded T-shirts that have an ice-cream logo on them. "Got a bunch of employee shirts for a place called Chunky Mike's."

Freddie pauses before the dresser mirror and points to a photo taped to the corner. "I bet this is her daughter. Looks to be . . . what? Eighteen? Twenty?"

I lean forward and study the photo. In it, Reese Bishop has her arms around the neck of a young woman who is laughing. The girl looks happy, as does Reese, and I feel a stab of jealousy at the maternal bond. Clearly, they are close. They love each other. Maybe this is what it looks like for an only child who doesn't have siblings to split the love with.

Freddie clicks his mouth. "There's a bunch more pictures here. Pretty girl." He is at her desk, and slides one of the photos leaning against a lamp to the center of the white-painted surface.

Pretty. I study the girl, who is standing on a lawn at some sort of outdoor concert or event. Her arms are spread out, a peek of her stomach showing, her grin wide, hair down, sunglasses perched on the top of her head.

"There's lotsa books here." He turns his head, studying the names on the spines of the paperbacks that are crammed into the bookshelf above her desk. "Novels, but some textbooks too. *US Politics and Procedures. Chemical Equations.* Looks like she's in college."

"We got a stat sheet on the victim?" I pull out my phone to check the case file. By now, we should have the background check, next of kin, public records, and . . . There's a new attachment. I tap the file. "Never mind, I got it."

I scroll through it. "Reese has a daughter named Jessica. Sophomore at UCLA. This is the address listed, so this has gotta be her room."

"Lives at home but hasn't reported her mom's body yet?" Freddie frowns. "Maybe she's out of town?"

"Or stays with a boyfriend." I glance at the collage of photos tacked on the wall above the desk. "See anyone who fits the bill?"

It takes a moment to look over them all. There are too many faces and too many photos. I'm not sure I could find even a handful of people I liked enough to take a photo with, and she has her arms wrapped around a few dozen.

I frown. "Not even a best friend," I muse. "Look at her in these photos. Notice anything?"

He leans forward and studies them, trying to see what I do, but I already know that he won't. A man could never understand all the dynamics that go into trying to survive as a young woman.

"I don't know," he finally says. "She's got nice teeth?"

"In all of these shots, she's the outsider." I study one of the photos, the girl perched on the end of a row, clinging to the group but not touching the blonde in front of her, like she doesn't want the girl to realize she's there. I remember that age. How awkward I felt, twenty pounds too heavy, my social circle interrupted by my time away, each interaction a minefield of saying or doing the wrong thing.

I hated that time. It was one of the reasons why I joined the police force. I wanted the built-in family, one that all wore the same thing and cared about the same objectives. Nothing to screw up there—except that I forgot I was a girl, and that alone made me a target in our trainee group.

Meeting Joe, talking to him . . . it had been a scuba tank of air at a time when I'd felt like I was drowning. He had pulled me to the surface, pulled me onto his raft and wrapped his arms around me, and from that day forth, I'd been in the sun. Warm. Confident. Safe.

Breathing.

There were a few photos of her with different guys, their arms slung around her neck or pulling her in a little too close. No love there. Only lust. Control. Use of a body before discarding it. Another feeling that was old yet familiar. I pull a Polaroid off the wall and hold it out to him. "What's your take on this? Boyfriend? Fling?"

He glances at it. "Fling. Or a friend with benefits."

I look over the rest of the photos, but they are more of the same. A girl ignored in the midst of a crowd. I could relate to that when I was her age, but unless she has her own dark secret that's built up her wall, our reasons are very different. Maybe she's emotionally stilted. Maybe she's a bitch.

I reattach the photo to the wall, and I hate the way the guy is looking at her. It's a sly look, the kind a fox would give its prey, and she's beaming. She probably slept with him and then he ditched her, his knife still stuck in her clueless heart.

I turn away from the wall. "Let's call her work. See what's up."

It takes less than an hour to confirm that she didn't show up for her shift this morning. I issue an APB, and Jessica Bishop officially becomes a missing person in Los Angeles County.

CHAPTER 6

DINAH

"You think the daughter is a killer or a victim?" Freddie sucks on the edge of a juice pouch as if he hasn't drunk anything in days. I look away before it seems like I'm staring.

"Neither," I say dryly. "There's not anything in there pointing to murder." I shift my position on the hard concrete step of Reese Bishop's porch, moving farther into the shade. "She was terminally ill. Overdose is a better way to cross over than hospice." It's not Freddie's fault that he doesn't see the writing on the wall. He's too young to understand making a decision like this.

I tap through the fields on the report, putting in details and dragging photos from the file to the appropriate locations. It's moments like this that I almost miss the paper forms. Almost.

"The daughter's culpability is just something we need to consider." He tilts his head back and empties the rest of the pouch into his mouth.

There is no *we*. This is my case, and tomorrow he will be back to whatever bullshit is on his training manifest. I swallow the thought and scroll past the area of the report where his information would be added.

"I promise to consider it as a possibility and see what the toxicology reports say." I click save.

"It's not a suicide. Not with the missing daughter." He crumples the juice container in both hands and looks around for a trash can. "Maybe she killed the mom and took off running? Or the killer offed the mom and snatched her? Or . . ." He perks up. "Maybe she found her mom dead and, like, had a mental breakdown?"

I fit the stylus into the holder at the top of the pad and lock the screen. "We don't even know for sure that Jessica is missing. City puts out three dozen APBs a day. Half the time the subject is just sitting at a bar around the corner, drunk. Trust me, Jessica could show up tomorrow off a flight from Cancún with a sunburn and a hangover."

He looks disappointed by the idea, and I remember what it was like to be a rookie detective. The craving of drama. The spotting of conspiracies. It isn't until you're seasoned that you realize conspiracies and complications only mean one thing: more paperwork and more loopholes for a ruthless defense attorney to jump through.

I stand and brush off the seat of my pants. "Well, the report is in. Thanks for your help today. Send over whatever you need me to fill out for your TO."

He pauses and has the indecency to look hurt. "What about the autopsy? That'll take, what? A few hours? I can meet back up with you when you get the call."

"Won't be necessary." I slide the pad into my bag. "I'll call you if there's anything strange."

He looks at his watch. "Okay, but I got three hours left on my shift."

"I'd call back to the station." I step off the porch. "Dispatch'll give you something to do."

He scowls and I'd forgotten the daily agony of babysitting a trainee. Thank God it wasn't my shit show. Ron and his wandering eyes could handle him.

I give Freddie a parting wave and a smile, grateful to have him out of my hair.

CHAPTER 7

JESSICA

I wake up in the dark. My arms are pinned to my sides, my head trapped in place with something, and there is a cool metal piece against either side of my cheeks.

I don't understand, and I press out with my legs and arms, trying to move, but I'm on my back and there's no give in these restraints.

This is a dream. It has to be. I— What did I do last night? Where did I go? Did I roll Molly again? Is that what this is? A bad trip? They say that every hit can be different, and the last two were good, so maybe I was due. I knew that asshole from Laguna was a mistake. That goofy grin, the way he tried to press my hand against his crotch before we even left the club.

Oh shit, I'm pissing. It's hot and wet and I can smell it. I pinch my lips shut and try to twist my face away, but I'm held in place by this thing, and I can feel the urine seeping into my underwear and God, I hope I'm not wearing that white leather skirt that I borrowed from that girl at work, she will absolutely kill me if I get pee all over that, and I can't believe I'm *still* peeing but oh my God, it feels so good to just let it out. My stomach cramp relaxes as my bladder empties, and I wonder how long I've been holding it.

I wet my lips and realize that I'm not wearing a gag, and if I make a noise, someone—maybe that asshole from Laguna . . . shit, what was his name? Maybe he'll hear me. I lick my lips again and try to scream, but only a hoarse yelp comes out. After swallowing, I try again.

This time my throat works, and I manage a shrill scream. I pause, waiting for the sound of steps, of someone rushing to save me, but there's nothing. I scream again, this one longer and louder, and from somewhere far away, her voice so faint I can barely hear it, another girl screams back.

It doesn't give me comfort, and this must definitely be a dream.

A nightmare.

CHAPTER 8

DINAH

The smell of the morgue still hangs from my hair when I walk into the middle of a standoff in my mother's kitchen. It's Isabel's birthday, and I know if I look in the fridge, there will be a three-layer carrot cake, because that's Izzy's favorite.

I set my gift, an iPhone rapid charger wrapped in metallic-blue paper with a white bow, on the counter next to a red gift bag that is definitely from Marci, who is too stingy to use more than one piece of tissue paper in a bag. I glance inside it. A book. A horrible gift for my dyslexic sister, even though Izzy will gush over it.

"I'm telling you that something's off." My brother, Sal, stands in the middle of the black-and-white-checkered tile, both hands on his hips, shoulders knotted back like he has a broomstick stuck through his elbows. "What is it? What aren't you telling us?"

My mother's house is a split-level ranch that was built in the '70s by our father, which means there isn't a single plumb line or outlet that doesn't occasionally spark. I ease around Sal to steal a fried drumstick off the pan on the stove. The theft earns a slap on my arm from our mother, who quickly follows up the action with a kiss on my cheek.

"Ma, you're not getting away with this." Sal gives me a one-armed hug while glaring at our mother.

"Oh, shush, you're paranoid!" She brushes him off with a wave of her hand and squeezes through the gap between the pantry door and the left end of the counter.

I watch her waddle toward the long dining table, and I try not to focus on her weight, which is getting worse each year. The obesity, paired with her refusal to take her blood pressure medication, is why she's been to the ER twice this year. It's a stress point in our already strained relationship, so I've stopped asking her about it.

"I'm not paranoid," Sal seethes. "Dinah, help me out with this. You can tell when someone's lying. You got that detective's intuition."

"It's true," Marci says, my sister's stick-thin body perched on the stool beside her brother, her forearms on the pale-yellow countertop. "Dani can always sniff out a lie."

Our eyes meet across the kitchen, and I know the statement isn't about the past, but it still feels like it is.

"You're calling your mother a liar? That's what my life has come down to? Forty-two years of raising you, and you call me a liar." Mom yanks the dish towel off the wall hook in disgust.

She's definitely lying. Sal's right about my intuition. I can spot deception at a hundred yards.

"He isn't calling you a liar." Izzy, who tenses at the mere idea of conflict despite being raised in a hot vat of it, pulls out a chair at the dining room table. I roll my eyes at her predictable support and catch Sal doing the same.

"Oh, bullshit," Sal insists. "Iz, don't let her play this 'woe is me' routine. That's a woman chest-deep in deceit. She thought she could sneak it past us, lie straight to our faces, and we wouldn't notice."

"They're chocolate chip cookies, Sal." Mom sniffs. "The same ones I've been making for thirty years."

I spot the cooling rack and take one of the crispier cookies, noticing that Sal hasn't let his suspicions stop him from eating at least six of them.

"They're tiny, flat pancakes of lies," he says, pointing to the pan of cookies as if it is a defendant in one of his jury trials.

I bite into the cookie and lean against the counter, my gaze connecting with Eric, Marci's husband, who hovers on the edge of the kitchen. You'd never know that he had been a soccer star in high school. That muscular, athletic build is now hidden beneath an extra forty pounds and a receding hairline.

I look away and realize Sal's right. There's something off about the taste. I bet it's nutmeg, an ingredient Mom's tried to sneak into her baking with increasing frequency despite our family's abhorrence to any sort of change in the status quo. Steven could go to jail, Izzy could be an alcoholic, I could be childless—but if the fucking tomato paste she uses in her spaghetti switches, our family implodes.

"Then don't eat them," Mom huffs, and when she collapses into the seat next to Izzy, the corners of her mouth tweak in a tiny smile. She knows damn well Sal will eat them. We all will.

That's the thing about her cookies. They are like Joe: imperfect in many ways but still irresistible.

My phone buzzes against my hip. I pull it out of the clip and open the text, which is from an unrecognized number.

It's Freddie. Got a copy of the autopsy results. Can we talk?

CHAPTER 9

DINAH

I chew on a second cookie as I climb the stairs to my mom's second floor, ignoring the neat waterfall of framed photos that cover the stairwell wall. As I climb higher, they transition from sepia photos of Mom and Dad's wedding and our early years to more recent ones: Our graduations, marriages. Baby photos of little Eric, Joleen Martha, Kaydence, Olivia, Maria, and Robert.

A burst of laughter comes from below, followed by a sharp remark from Sal, who was likely the brunt of the joke. I swallow the bite and pull my phone out of my pocket, rereading Freddie's text.

It's Freddie. Got a copy of the autopsy results. Can we talk?

What was there to talk about? I'd been at the autopsy, and it was clean and uneventful. No sign of trauma, nothing to point to anything other than an overdose.

I close Freddie's text and call Joe, pinning the phone against my ear as I pass Mom's bedroom, the tiny hall bath, and Sal and Steven's old room. The door at the end of the hall is closed, and I quicken my pace, wanting privacy before my husband answers.

I turn the brass knob and slip inside the dark bedroom, quietly closing the door as Joe's voicemail comes on.

I wait for his automation to end, then speak.

"Hey. I'm at my mom's. Are you on the way? Call me back." I sound both irritated and needy, which is a mistake. I'm not needy, and I know he's busy. It's my family that's the problem. The looks they give me when he is late. The repeated questions about where he is and when he will arrive. *Should we wait for Joe to eat? How often does he work late? It's a Saturday; why is he meeting with clients?*

They don't understand, and I refuse to discuss it with them. Joe's work is often the difference between a client's survival and death. The right psychiatrist can be a lifeline that turns their future in a new direction, assuming they are willing to listen.

Sometimes they aren't, especially the patients who are committed against their will.

Those are the patients who scare me and attract him. Maybe they scare me because they attract him. I want him to love his job; I just don't want him to love it more than me.

I sit on my bed and stare at Marci's side. Our room is a time capsule of the 2000s. A poster of Freddie Prinze Jr. is tacked to the wall, surrounded by Polaroids of her and her friends. They had invaded this room, sprawling over the space with no regard to Marci's dorky big sister. I'd put on my headphones and pretend not to hear the snide comments they'd make about me as they watched episodes of *The Real World* and painted their nails.

When they weren't around, she was the perfect little sister. Just eighteen months my junior and a patient recipient of the advice and secrets I had to share. It's embarrassing, looking back, how I craved her attention, even if it only came when none of the cool girls were watching.

I had loved having a little sister. I still remember how big her eyes got when I told her about my first kiss. She was the one—the only one—I told about my first crush, and how he had given me his letterman jacket after the game and let me keep it for the weekend. We had giggled over it together, each of us trying it on, and sniffed the dirty lining and convinced ourselves it smelled heavenly.

She was the only one I told about the night after Dad's promotion, when he got too drunk at the bar around the corner, and Mom got pissed and made him sleep on the couch, and I babysat the Kellen kids and didn't get back until almost midnight.

Maybe I shouldn't have told her about that. Maybe she was too young. If I could rewind the clock, I wouldn't have said a thing. I wouldn't have given her that secret. Because now she has it, forever, and I have nothing to even out the scale. Nothing but hatred over what she did while I was gone.

We were supposed to be sisters. Supposed to fight for each other. Supposed to be loyal to each other. That's what families do—at least, that's what I had always been told they do. Then again, my mother didn't fight for or protect me, so maybe the concept of family is bullshit and Joe is lucky he's an only child.

In comparison to Marci's colorful side of the room, mine is stark and boring. It always has been, even before I was sent away. Other than my bed, with its plain navy spread and gray-striped pillows, there's just my desk, a shelf of books, and a tower of dusty CDs. On the wall are my plaques from our school's awards nights. Valedictorian. Honors. Science Fair Finalist. Scholarship Recipient.

At one point, I was on track for UCLA or Stanford. But when I missed the summer before my senior year and the following fall semester, my GPA tanked, along with my college prospects. I lost my class rank, my spot in social standing, and my ability to wear a bikini without wincing in shame.

Marci's friends termed it a mental breakdown; that's what they whispered and laughed over, and she let them do it. She let them think whatever they wanted, because she was too busy with her new boyfriend to care. And maybe she wouldn't have cared anyway.

When I was finally allowed to come back, I had a suitcase full of dirty clothes and big plans to put everything behind me and jump back into my old life. She killed that possibility as soon as I walked into our room.

I dropped my purse on the floor and spotted her homecoming dance photo, framed and on the dresser in plain sight, like it wasn't a knife to my heart. His letterman jacket hung over the back of her desk chair.

I'd been gone six months, and she had swooped in on my first love and sucked him into her orbit. Goodbye, nerdy and innocent Dinah. Hello, popular and beautiful Marci.

Looking back, I never had a chance.

My phone buzzes with another text.

Where are you? Call me to discuss the autopsy.

I sigh and call Freddie, wondering how he got a copy of the report.

CHAPTER 10

JESSICA

The overhead light comes on, and there's a doctor standing by the door, his hand on the switch. I stop screaming, silenced by the view of the room. I try to look to the right, then the left. Oh, thank God. It's a hospital room, not a torture chamber. I'm latched to a gurney, which is so much better than *The Princess Bride* Bed of a Thousand Souls or whatever it was called.

Still mildly alarming, though.

"You don't need to scream." The doctor takes a clipboard from a hook by the door. "If you scream, you're going to hurt your throat and you're going to be dehydrated. There's nothing here to fear. Are you in any pain?"

Am I in pain? I strain forward in an attempt to see the rest of my body, but I can't see past my boobs.

He approaches, peering at me. "I need to know if you're in any pain."

"No." I clear my throat, and the action causes me to start hacking.

He waits for my coughing to pass. He's not bad looking. My mom dated a doctor last year, and that guy looked like a wrinkly potato with a giant nose. She'd called him "nice looking," but that was a load of fresh bullshit. Maybe his bank account was nice looking.

This guy has a nice bank account, if the Rolex on his wrist is any clue.

"My name is Joe Marino. You can call me Dr. Joe. I'm the head of medicine here."

Here. His lab coat has some sort of monogram on it, but I can't tell what it says.

"You were pretty out of it when you came in." He writes something on his clipboard. "Feel like talking right now? It'd be great to get some more information from you."

"Sure." I can't even nod in this thing. My wrists are sweating, and that's a first for me.

"Name?" He moves the pen to a new spot on the paper and waits.

I pause. Frown.

My name.

Okay, I know this. Two words. Maybe three. Louisa May Alcott has three.

"You might not remember it," he says casually, like it's normal for someone to forget their name. "You're potentially experiencing some short-term memory loss, which is common after a traumatic event."

"Did I *have* a traumatic event?" I must have, unless this is the normal sleeping arrangement in this place.

"Well, something was traumatic enough for you to admit yourself. Do you remember what you told us when you came in?"

I admitted myself? I stare blankly at him and try to remember, but the last I recall, I was eating dinner. I made chicken alfredo, one of those frozen, just-dump-a-bag-into-a-skillet-and-stir things. It wasn't great. Kind of rubbery. Mom had said it was good.

Oh, she'll know my name. Hers too. Right now, all I can lock in to is that she had brown hair. Her face is just a big blur, like someone rubbed over it with an eraser.

"Focus, please." He waves his hand to catch my attention. "Do you remember what you told us when you came in? What you'd done?"

What you'd done. I didn't like the sound of that. It wasn't just the words; it was the way he said it, like he was accusing me of something. What I'd done . . . What could I have possibly done?

Missed my shift, probably. If that wasn't it then, it definitely was now. My shift at . . . I blink.

"Do you remember?"

I try to shake my head no, but the brace around my head pins it in place. "No. Can you get me out of this thing? I peed on myself."

"Avoiding the reality won't make it go away."

This is ridiculous. I just told him that I *peed* on myself, which is really embarrassing to admit.

"I'll help you deal with it. That's my job. It's what I do."

"Can your job be to untie my hands? I really need to scratch my nose." I flap my hands against the bed.

"Why don't you tell me what happened last night?" He sits on the edge of the bed, and I don't like the press of his butt against my leg.

I try to move it away but can't. "I ate chicken alfredo."

"Okay, chicken alfredo." He writes that down. "What else?"

"There was broccoli in it."

He just looks at me, his pen's tip still against the page. "Did anyone eat dinner with you?"

"Yeah, my mom."

"You live with your mom?"

Do I live with my mom? God, I hope not. I'm like . . . Shit. How old am I? I growl in frustration. I need a mirror. If I could look in a mirror, I'd know my freaking name. My age. My living situation. "Do you have a mirror?"

"Okay, we'll stop for today, sound good?" He moves to his feet and checks a bag of fluids that is hanging off a stand to my right.

"No, wait. I can remember." I pinch my eyes closed and try to grab on to something, anything. I was hiking in the woods. Another memory of a little dog, something gray, in my lap. We were speeding to help it. All useless memories. I don't even know who "we" are.

"It's okay." He pulls something out of his pocket—a syringe—and inserts it into a port on the side of the line running to my hand. "It's common for these memories to come back in a day or so. Rest up and I'll check back in with you."

"But I peed my pants," I say weakly. It feels like something that should matter.

He doesn't respond, just hangs up the clipboard and flicks off the light switch. Everything goes dark except for him, outlined in the light from the door.

"Sleep," he orders.

CHAPTER 11

DINAH

"Dinah?" Freddie sounds surprised, like he didn't just tell me to call him.

"Yes, it's me," I snap. Downstairs, the front door slams shut, and the entire frame of Mom's house shudders in response. I move to the window and push the faded-red curtain to the side, hoping to see Joe's SUV.

"They sent me the autopsy results."

"Yes, I know. You texted me about it. I was there for it, so I'm a step ahead of you."

"Yeah. So, it says Reese Bishop still had three or four months to live."

I blow out a breath, annoyed with this conversation. He was a trainee not assigned to this case, someone who shouldn't have even received the autopsy report. "Okay, so?"

"So, why kill herself now? Why not wait and live a little longer?"

"Have you ever been terminally ill, Freddie?" Joe's vehicle isn't on the street, but from this vantage point I can see as my younger sister steps off the porch and walks down the driveway, her phone to her ear. I slowly move the handle of the window crank, opening it until I can hear the faint sound of her voice.

". . . told you that. We're about to eat."

"Well, no," Freddie says. "But—"

"Maybe she didn't want to move into hospice, didn't want to have a heart attack at work, didn't want to become a burden to her family. Is this the only thing you don't like about the autopsy? That her expiration date was too far out for you?" I hiss the words, not wanting my conversation to carry down to Marci.

"Well, that's a rather crass way to put it," he says diplomatically, and I bet this guy listens to self-help podcasts and cold plunges each morning.

I close my eyes and tell myself to chill. *He's a baby,* I remind myself. When I was his age, I found everything suspicious. Everything. Even the things that were just normal human behavior, like a newlywed husband who worked late every night yet never answered his office line. Being suspicious doesn't mean you're valid.

It doesn't matter if Reese Bishop had four months left to live. Sometimes people want to die. Sometimes they need help. That's what this is, period. As much as this trainee would love a juicy murder investigation, our job is to verify the suicide and move on so this is cleared from Rita's desk by the time she returns from maternity leave.

If I didn't hate Ron Memphis so much, I'd call and tell him to get this guy to back off and focus on parking-ticket warrants or something else that's light-years away from this case. "Look, Freddie. We're good. Focus on other things. We'll wait on toxicology and see if the daughter shows up in the next forty-eight hours. We have her credit cards flagged and the APB out. A traffic cam or something will catch her car. She'll move and we'll get her."

"Toxicology takes weeks. We don't want this to go cold."

There it is again. *We.* Is this how they do it in Montebello? Let rookies run apeshit? I inhale deeply and force myself to count to five before responding. "Freddie, other than you really wanting this to be a murder, what evidence is there? Forced entry? Sign of a struggle? Insurance money? Motive?"

There is silence on his end, just like I knew there would be. No. The answers are no, no, no, no. We need at least three of the four in order to get a warrant, and more stacked on that in order to get the DA to approve an arrest and go after a conviction.

I'd gone over Reese's scene with a fine-tooth comb, and there was nothing there that pointed to murder. Nothing.

"Maybe there's no forced entry or sign of a struggle because it was the daughter."

I shake my head. "It wasn't the daughter. Matricide is a one-in-a-million statistic. It doesn't happen."

"Yeah, well. I don't like the missing daughter," he says stubbornly. "No credit card activity in over forty-eight hours—that's strange."

"What about the daughter's phone?" It's a question I already know the answer to, but if he wants to chase a dead lead, I'll at least point out the holes for him.

"Its location is turned off, but it's got data pings all over. It's on the move, but it's odd activity. I'm not certain it wasn't dumped somewhere."

For a patrol officer, this guy has a lot of opinions.

"She's not a seasoned criminal, Freddie. She's twenty years old. She's not dumping her cell, at least not intentionally. Maybe she lost it, or it was stolen, or she's couch surfing with friends."

"It's a lot of *maybes*."

"Okay, so let's talk through the major ones," I concede. Below me, Marci glances toward the house and then walks quickly down the driveway, her phone still stuck to her ear.

I lean forward, wondering who she's talking to. "We have a missing girl with a dead mom. Option A: she has no idea what's happened and is off doing something. Which, I agree with you, isn't likely but something we should still consider."

He grunts and I pull the curtains closed, interrupting the distraction. "Option B: she found or watched her mom do it, freaked out, and ran. Also fairly unlikely, though grief does strange things to people—"

"Option C," he interrupts. "She killed her and ran."

God, this guy is morbid. I make a face. "Right. And . . . option D: someone else killed Reese, then killed or took Jessica."

"Yes," he confirms, though what exactly he's confirming, I'm not sure. "What are you doing right now?" he asks.

"I'm at a birthday party over in Glendale."

"Want to skip out on it and go over the crime scene photos? We could meet at Baby's in an hour."

I haven't been to Baby's Coffee in weeks and weaken at the thought of their iced latte. But as much as I'd love to run from my family and their questions, there's still a chance Joe will show up. I have to stay.

"No, I need to be here for a few hours." I glance at the white bedside clock, its red numbers still an hour off, even two decades later. "I'll call you in the morning. Maybe we can meet up then."

"Awesome," he responds.

I grimace but say nothing. As if in response, my call-waiting beeps in. It's Joe.

CHAPTER 12

DINAH

Joe arrives, all smiles and apologies and with a present for Izzy, which I hadn't asked him for but am not surprised by. My husband always remembers things. Every anniversary, every to-do item, every misstep.

There's an encyclopedia inside that head of his, with a heading and tab for each subject. His Dinah section could encompass three volumes, and includes every conversation we've ever had, any story I've shared, successes I've had, mistakes I've made. My preferences, my health details, my shortcomings and flaws. He loves it all, the good and bad parts of me, and while most husbands bitch about their wives' shortcomings, Joe would never speak negatively about me to someone else. It's one of the promises of our marriage, one I obey as staunchly as he does.

Of course, my biggest flaw—the fact that several chapters of his Dinah encyclopedia are all lies—is the one flaw he'll never discover. A secret worth killing for.

Isabel takes Joe's gift into the living room and sits on the couch, opening the small, perfectly wrapped box. It's a pair of saltwater pearl earrings, and she stares down at them, her mouth open in shock. When she finally looks up, her gaze darts to me. "Th-they're beautiful," she stammers. "But too generous, Joe. Honestly."

In the best brother-in-law race, Joe just increased his lead. I'm certain Eric didn't get anything for her, certainly not anything like this. Joe walks up behind me and wraps his arms around my waist. I tilt my head back, and he presses a kiss on my lips, then refocuses on Izzy. "You lost a pair like that a few years ago—in South Carolina, right? On your honeymoon?"

"How did you know?" Izzy pulls one pearl free from the velvet and works it through the tender lobe of her ear.

"You mentioned it at Christmas, when you told the story about the roller coaster."

If she did, I don't remember it. But again, that is Joe. On our first date, I asked our waitress for no avocados or carrots on my Cobb salad, and just last week, he got me a to-go order from Elmo's Garden and ordered one just like that, even though we've been married for eight years and I haven't eaten a Cobb salad since our first date.

Joe sits down next to Izzy and asks her about her job and if she is still working with isotope permutations. She launches into a yawn-worthy explanation of her newest findings, and I excuse myself and go into the kitchen, where Sal is standing with Eric, a beer in one hand, chocolate chip cookie in the other. My brother's earlier accusations don't seem to be an issue as cookie crumbs spray out of his mouth.

"Grab me another beer," he says as soon as I open the fridge. "So, this prick asks me for a continuance—*me*—and I said, 'Fuck you and your deadbeat client.' Said that to him right to his face."

I have no doubt he did. Sal, bless his soul, was one of the only people who stuck up for me after my social exile. He was only thirteen, but he punched Gary McKeegan in the nose for writing *Dinah Franzeta is a fat slob* on the bathroom wall, then told him he'd face-fuck his mother if he ever said my name again.

Sal was five inches shorter than Gary, with arms barely bigger than broomsticks. The senior carried him above his head through the halls and tossed him in the cafeteria dumpster, then leaned in and punched him in the mouth. Sal had his jaw wired shut for five weeks while it healed.

I grab Sal a Budweiser and two bottles of Guinness for Joe and myself. After shutting the fridge, I pass Sal's bottle to him, kiss him on the cheek, then use the opener on the wall to pop the Guinness caps.

My brother is already on his verbal victory lap as I ease around him and return to the living room, where Izzy is laughing at something my husband has said. Joe turns to watch me enter, and I take the seat next to him and pass him his beer. He clinks his bottle against mine, and the memory of my first beer pushes, uninvited, into my head.

Shhhh. I don't want anyone to hear us. Just take a small sip and see if you like it. There.

A stupid decision, that first sip. Then the next, then the next. A few pebbles that caused an avalanche.

They took me away on a Tuesday morning, right after everyone boarded the bus for school and my father left for work. He didn't say anything to me on his way out. His face was stone, his steps quick, and his gaze swept everywhere but in my direction.

Then it was just me and my mother, waiting for the van, her mouth tight and drawn, her arms tightly crossed over her chest, just in case I tried to hold her hand.

When they drove me away, I watched her out the window, hoping she would change her mind, would call them back—would give me a hug, if nothing else.

She didn't even wait for the van to round the corner. She speed-walked back into the house and shut the door.

There had been no beer after that. My diet had been strictly regulated, as had every other aspect of my life. No more hidden moments. No secrets. No privacy. On my first night there, I was stripped naked, my legs pulled apart, a stranger's face between them.

I take a small sip, but my stomach revolts at the taste. Joe reaches out and grips my hand, his touch warm.

So much love between us. The relationship I've always dreamed of come to life.

But he can never find out the truth of that year.

CHAPTER 13

JOE

My wife thinks she's so smart with her little red wagon full of secrets. She pulls it behind her closely, picking up different deceptions as she goes and adding them to the mound that weighs down the bed. Initially, there were only a few, but as the years have passed, she's gotten bolder. With each seemingly undiscovered lie or omission, she digs another hole in her grave, but she doesn't know that. She thinks she's crafty. She covets that red wagon of lies; it's her comfort blanket, her proof that she has the upper hand in our marriage, that she's not the boring woman her sisters are—she can't possibly be, because look at this and that and this.

I understand her far better than she understands herself, which is a good thing. She'll never see how broken she is, won't fully appreciate that I'm still here despite all those broken pieces. My wife is my favorite puzzle to put together, and sometimes I like to rearrange the pieces of her mind just to keep it fresh.

Maybe one day I'll break her in the process, but I doubt it. She's a fighter, like me. A lover and a fighter, all rolled into one fucked-up enigma.

I wouldn't want her any other way.

CHAPTER 14

DINAH

Baby's Coffee is full, as it always is. The eclectic family-owned spot is a combination grocery store and coffee shop, with a dark roast that manages to be both strong and smooth. They also give free drinks to anyone in uniform, which is why I pass three badges on the way in. I text Joe while in line and order an iced coffee with toasted marshmallow, cold foam, and two Splendas.

Freddie is sitting at a sunlit table by the window, his attention on his department-issued tablet. He's wearing a hunter-green sweat suit, and looks up at my approach and smiles, showing off all those white teeth.

I take the seat opposite him. "Morning."

"Okay, so I've been digging into the daughter."

Not what I wanted to hear. He should be doing ride-alongs with his TO and case studies on cold files. Anything other than digging into this. I force a smile. "Good morning, Freddie. I'm good, thank you."

He pauses. There're already two empty coffee cups in front of him. "Hi. Good morning. You need me to wait until you get your coffee, or can I start?"

I smile despite myself. "Go ahead."

"Okay, so we're dealing with a smart girl. Dean's list. Has worked a job since she was fourteen. Street and book smart, according to everything I've found."

I'm not surprised, but I bite my tongue and nod. "Okay. What else?"

"No boyfriend, though she's got a lot of admirers, if you know what I mean." He raises his brows.

"No, I don't know what you mean," I drawl. "You're saying she dated around?"

He shrugs. "Just my observation. She was a partier. Not hard core, but a girl with a busy social calendar."

"Where are you getting that info? Her socials?"

"She had a warning citation for underage drinking at Venice Beach two years ago. I sent her pic over to a few cops I know who work the clubs and that scene. One said he's seen her hanging out at the door to the EMD club, talking up the DJs, when he worked security there."

The citation is something I should have turned up, but I didn't want to do a search on her too early and hadn't thought about running one in the last twenty-four hours, what with the autopsy and Izzy's party and overall status of upheaval that my life was currently in.

He hunches over the pad and swipes his finger over the screen. "I was thinking we could stop by her job, talk to her coworkers. Get her peers' opinions."

I try not to sigh, but the exasperation still wheezes out of me. "Don't you have other things to do? Is Ron still in the hospital?"

He grins. "Sick of me?"

Yes. "I don't need help on this, Freddie. I got it."

"Well, Ron's still out of commission, so I've got nothing but time." He rubs his palms together like that's a good thing.

The barista calls my name and I immediately stand, grateful for the interruption. I take my time picking up my cup and stopping by the stand to get a straw and a napkin. I glance at Freddie; his knee is bouncing, his whole body wired and ready for action.

As soon as I retake my seat, he pounces back into the conversation.

"You pull up SMED on her?" His forehead is dotted with sweat, and I wonder how many shots of espresso he's had.

I remove the lid and use the straw to stir the cold foam into the drink. "District attorney hasn't approved it yet." Probably because I just this morning submitted the request. SMED is an online database for law enforcement, one that monitors internet chatter and so-called private communications through different social media networks and chat rooms. It's an enormous invasion of privacy, but one that's afforded to law enforcement in cases where the individual is at serious risk. "If the APB doesn't find her by tomorrow, I'll probably get it."

"If this is sex trafficking, tomorrow's going to be too late."

I watch as a girl at the table beside us takes a photo of her drink. "I don't like trafficking for this. The mom is too messy. Jessica is either involved or oblivious. You still watching her cell activity?"

"Yeah. Pinging all over town."

"I've left her two messages, but she hasn't returned my calls." I reattach the lid and pierce the straw through the top. "She could be on a bender."

"Shitty thing to come home to—crime scene tape and a lock on the front door."

"Better than finding your mom like that."

My phone rings and I flinch at the sound, quickly silencing the device as I look at the screen. It's the coroner's office. I hold up a finger to Freddie. "I've got to take this. Give me a minute."

I answer the call and press the phone to my ear, zigzagging quickly through the tables and out the side door. "Marino."

"This is Dr. Pulle, with the coroner's office." Her voice is crisp. There isn't any love lost between me and the older woman. She likes dead bodies a little too much, in my opinion. Then again, I've never met a coroner who didn't give me the ick.

"Hi, Doc." I stop in the shade of the awning. "You got something?"

"It's about Reese Bishop, something that occurred to me after I wrapped the autopsy."

"What's that?"

Sheila Pulle is not an idiot, and I listen as she shares a bit of information that would make Freddie backflip with joy and spawn at least five new conspiracy theories. I twist in place, making sure Freddie is still at our table. He is, his attention on his phone, his tall frame slumped in his seat. In his sweatshirt and pants, you'd never know he was a cop.

"I heard there's an APB out on the daughter, so I thought it might be pertinent," Dr. Pulle finishes.

"Yeah, absolutely." I nod. "Thanks for the call. I appreciate it."

"I can amend the autopsy report to include this."

"No need. I'll put a note in the file and dig into it on my end. Find out what I can about the daughter's history. It might be nothing, but it might be something. You know how those things go."

"Yeah. Okay."

I end the call and take a moment to digest the information. Freddie looks up from his phone, and our gaze connects through the glass. I lift my chin and then gesture with my head, beckoning him outside. He stands and grabs my cup as a group of college girls pounce on our table.

He doesn't need to know this. It might be the missing piece to this puzzle, but it would toss him a bone and he's already overly attached to this case.

I need a different bone—one I can throw in the opposite direction.

CHAPTER 15

DINAH

I don't know what normal married couples talk about at dinner, but I imagine the meal stretches on interminably. One spouse picks up their phone, the other follows suit, and the silence is filled with short video clips, the quiet tap of fingers against glass, the chime of points being scored on an app. Occasionally, the clink of silverware against china, the murmur of a question—*Do you want another glass of wine? Need more potatoes? Does the chicken seem dry?*

Then at some point, the event ends. One person rises to carry their plate to the sink, the other follows.

I don't ever want that. It's important to me that we are a linked pair, tied to each other with our love and our secrets. A relationship should have consequences upon dissolution. The steeper the consequences, the stronger the connection. For Joe and me, either of us could drown the other with just a few words, and that awareness heightens the frequency of the electricity between us.

Now, over our dinner of roast duck and wild rice, our attention rarely strays from each other. Conversation flows back and forth quickly, each of us anxious to reply to the other, our words often rushing together as we finish each other's sentences and, just as often, burst into laughter. We discuss a novel we are both reading, the stray cat who keeps lingering around, and the new chardonnay we picked up last week. We hem and haw over whether to see a play that is opening next weekend and whether we should fire our pest exterminator.

We are in love with being in love, and we have been this way going on a decade.

It is, as my mother says, an enigma. Couples don't stay in love, she preaches. It's a lot of work, she declares.

It isn't a lot of work. It's fun. He's the best part of my life, and I'm the best part of his. It's not by accident; it's because I strive to make it so. I work my ass off to be the best part of his day, every day, without fail.

Joe asks how work is going, and I tell him bits and pieces of my week, strategically avoiding the mention of the clingy trainee, whom I will aggressively push back to Ron on Monday. By then, he should be released from the hospital and back at home. Freddie isn't worth mentioning to Joe, because his involvement will be over in a matter of days. Just one or two more meetups, and then we'll be done. The chief will sign off on Reese Bishop's suicide, and the daughter will become just one more missing girl in a city that swallows them for breakfast.

I ask Joe about his classes and his students, and he tells me a funny story about a campus parking attendant. We talk about the center and a few patients he's struggling with.

We discuss this upcoming weekend and our plans to spend it at the farm. We have a new mower that he'll use on the fields. I want to work in the greenhouse and have a crochet throw I plan on curling up in the hammock with and finishing.

As we talk, warmth fills my chest. Is it wrong to swoon at our age?

We don't do the dishes; I used paper plates, so we dump them into the trash. Then he heads to the clinic and I escape to my office, where I pull up the DA's response to my inquiry.

She granted access to SMED.

I enter my credentials and dive into Jessica Bishop's private life.

CHAPTER 16

DINAH

Jessica: Started my period. Guess you're in the clear.

    Ian: Good. We're having a party on Saturday if you want to stop by. If you're off the rag by then, come find me there.

    Jessica: Nah, I'm good.

    Ian: Don't be a bitch. Stop by and have a beer.

———

Mom: can you stop by Ralph's on the way home? I have a prescription that needs to be picked up.

    Jessica: sure

    Mom: thanks. Also, please grab some half and half and onion salt.

    Jessica: Ok

———

@Jessbesslikesamess liked a status

@Jessbesslikesamess commented "haha, ikr?"

@Jessbesslikesamess commented "okay whatever"

@Jessbesslikesamess saved a post

@Jessbesslikesamess commented "omg I want one so bad"

@Jessbesslikesamess commented "I heard they're closing it on the 14th. My friend works there, so it's legit."

@Jessbesslikesamess sent a friend request to Ellie Histick

SMED is like digging through someone's underwear drawer—a very deep underwear drawer where you have to sift through backyards of sand for each find. Over 70 percent of all internet activity is part of the database. Lots of sand.

For Jessica Bishop, there are over fourteen million entries. It's not terrible. I've dealt with cases that had a hundred million and more. As a fresh pot of coffee brews, I create a flag for communication related to her mother and use it to notate anything that might hint at their relationship.

It doesn't take long to see that they were close. I yawn as I go through their texts, which make up an almost constant stream of check-ins, questions, and boring back-and-forth.

Reading it all is like eavesdropping on a conversation with Marci and my mother. All happiness and hearts. *Oh, I love you so much. Oh, I love you. See you in a few hours. I can't wait! Counting the hours.* Blah, blah, blah, blah, blah.

I didn't have this with our mother. The hard right turn my life took at sixteen . . . that severed the lifeline between us. She wrote me off after that, and I'm still raw and hurt over how my entire family handled the fallout.

Is that how you treat someone you love? Is that what love from a parent looks like?

I mentally divorced my family after that, at least as much as a good Italian girl could. We have all the appearances in place now, but I know, behind the hugs and the kisses, the weekly dinners and the friendly chastising, how fragile my connection with them really is.

Paper thin. Douse it in water or blood, and you could break it with one gentle poke of your finger.

Was Jessica and Reese's the same?

I scroll through the texts and click on a photo Reese sent Jessica. It's a plate of brownies, a heart carved in the top of one. The message sent with the photo: Made these for you. Good luck with tomorrow's civics exam!

I pinch my lips together and move on.

Joe once published an article on the unhealthy effects of a parent-child bond that is too strong, especially once the child reaches adulthood. His research is deep and well documented. Adults who are still dependent on and connected to their parents experience problems in their own marriages, poor connections with their own children, and a reduced ability to think and problem-solve for themselves.

A pair of headlights sweeps over my office window. After locking the computer screen, I close my notebook and slide it into the desk drawer. Pushing away from the desk, I stand and collect my coffee cup.

I flip off the room's light switch and head downstairs to greet my husband.

CHAPTER 17

JESSICA

My hands are free. That's the first thing I notice when I wake up.

I lie there for a moment, testing my movement. My legs are also unshackled, as is my head. I roll to my side, and the pain in my back weakens. I slowly slide my hands underneath me and push up into a seated position and look around.

The hospital room is empty except for my bed and a plastic table and chair in the corner.

"Hello?" The room doesn't have a window, not even on the door, and the walls are like the dog shelter I volunteer at in the summers—stainless steel on the bottom half so we can easily spray them down with bleach. The top half is padded. I saw walls like this in a movie once. It was about a girl in a mental institution, and I let that detail fester in my head for a moment.

Is that what this is? A mental institution? The idea is so absurd that I let out a laugh, then stop at the thought that I'm alone in a room, laughing, and that fits right in with the motif.

Maybe I *am* in a mental institution. If so, it's probably the one just off 60, right before I-5. I used to pass that one every time I went downtown, though there are probably dozens in LA. I'm definitely not in one of the fancy ones, though that would actually be kinda cool, and my best chance to meet and befriend a celebrity.

I swing my legs over the side of the bed and test my weight. They feel like spaghetti, so I give myself a moment and roll my neck and stretch my left arm back behind my head by its elbow, then do the same with the right. If Mom were here, she'd massage out the cluster of knots in between my shoulder blades. Without her, I try my best to open up my back by stretching my arm across my chest.

I wonder if they've called her. Maybe she's in the lobby, waiting for me with a big bouquet of balloons. She loves balloons, even though they are the most useless and annoying gift on the planet. She's threatened to have balloons at my wedding, like all over the place. A sea of them.

Do you remember what you told us when you came in? What you'd done?

I still don't even know why I'm here. Am I sick? Injured? Maybe I have the same pulmonary disease Mom has and I collapsed or something. I think of her on the sidewalk by our house, gasping for breath, her eyes open wide, her hand weak when I held it.

I'd known right then, before all the tests and the ER visits and the specialists, that she was going to die. It was this gut punch that occurred, a flip of a switch where everything was okay in my life, and then it was all just a countdown of moments we had remaining.

I pinch my eyes closed and try to think of her phone number. It's in my cell, and I haven't had to type out the numbers in ages. I'm sure she's wondering where I am. Probably thinks I'm at a guy's house, though the current loser hasn't returned my texts in like a week.

I tuck my hair behind my ear; it's ridiculously greasy. I don't think it's ever been this oily in my entire life. Suddenly, the need to wash it is unbearable. My scalp itches, so I use my nails to dig into it but can't deal with the slick rub on my fingers.

I stop and stare at the insides of my arms.

I have bandages on both wrists.

Another mystery. Did I struggle so much with my restraints that I damaged the skin? My wrists do feel sore. I pull up one pant leg of the pale-green medical scrubs I'm wearing to see if the same bandages are on my ankles. They aren't—my ankles look just fine.

The IV is still in the back of my right hand, the end capped off and taped down. I leave it alone, ignoring the dull pain radiating out from the needle. I'm not adept or prepared enough to try to remove my own IV. I pulled at my mom's drain line once, trying to help her get it out, and fainted dead away when a bit of fatty tissue came out with it. I came to flat on my back on the bathroom floor, with her in a giggling fit beside me, the drain line still hanging out of her body.

I wonder how far away the waiting room is and if it's on this floor. Mom shouldn't sit out there too long. She needs to be at home, relaxing in her chair, *Golden Girls* on the TV. I might be here for a few more hours, and it's going to stress me out if I know she's out there in some uncomfortable chair, waiting on me.

The bandages on my wrists are annoying, and I pick at the left one, using my dominant hand to peel away the edge. It's a slow process. The skin revealed is bright red and inflamed. They probably don't know it, but I have a skin allergy to certain adhesives, and it looks like the one they've used is one of the ones I can't have.

I pause, the top half of the bandage free, and look for a nurse's call button. There's got to be one somewhere. I examine the sides of the bed, but this is a super-basic one. It doesn't even have the up or down buttons, or any power at all. Honestly, this place seems kind of shitty, which does sort of track with the outside of the building, if it's the one by I-5.

I stand, testing my legs, then do a very slow circle around the room. There's nothing here. Literally just my bed and this seating area, which has that same rounded thick-plastic look that you see on kindergarten playgrounds. What's really odd is that there's no bathroom. I don't understand what I'll do when I have to go, especially since there's no nurse's call button for help. No wonder I peed on myself earlier. My underwear still feels damp, which is like an infection waiting to happen.

I sit on the plastic chair and lay my left arm on the table, using the flat surface to finish getting this bandage off. Twice in the process, my hair falls in my eyes, and twice I have to tuck it behind my ear, and I swear I'd use the last water bottle in existence to rinse it out if I could. I can't believe I slept on a pillowcase with this greasy head. My face is going to break out like crazy, especially since I haven't washed it either.

What I don't understand is how long I've been here. This feels like days of oil in my hair, maybe a week of it. Have I been sleeping more than I think I have? Because I have a day's worth of memories, at most. I remember seeing the doctor. A few times where I woke up in the restraints. And today.

Either way, the very first thing I'll do when I walk in the house is take a shower. Maybe I'll splurge and use some of those coconut salt scrubs Mom ordered from Florida and do like a whole spa thing with lit candles.

It sounds heavenly, and I smile, rubbing at my raw skin to keep from scratching it. Neosporin—that's another thing the nurse needs to bring. Neosporin and a different type of bandage, and to remove this IV and check on my mom . . . I need a piece of paper so I can keep track of all this. There's no way I'm going to remember it. Right now, my head feels like it's stuffed with cotton balls, like I'm having the world's worst hangover.

I need to stop doing Molly. Travis says it kills brain cells, which absolutely seems accurate, but shit, I love the high. I love the laughter. I never laugh like that except when I'm on it.

I have an itch in my side, and when I go to scratch it, I feel a fabric band around my waist. Pulling up my shirt, I stare down, confused.

I'm wearing diapers. White, stretchy pull-up-style diapers. Not wet panties—a wet diaper. And that's apparently how I'm supposed to do the deed.

Well, that ain't happening. I'm not pissing on myself again, not now that I'm awake.

I return to working on the bandage, and when it's finally off, I try to understand what I'm seeing. Two deep cuts, running from my wrist joints to halfway down my forearm. Not horizontal. I remember learning in seventh grade from Spencer Barnes that suicide attempts should never go left to right, but up and down so you open more blood vessels or something like that.

I know what this is, but it—even more so than me being in this room—doesn't make any sense.

Why would I try to kill myself?

CHAPTER 18

DINAH

I eat my cereal and ignore my phone, which is lighting up with texts from Freddie. Joe enters the kitchen, and I turn it over on the table so he won't see the notifications.

"Morning." My husband is wearing his charcoal suit today, the one with pale-blue pinstripes that are so faint you can only see them close up. I love that suit; it fits his build perfectly and highlights the bit of gray that is beginning to appear in his hair.

I can't wait for him to go fully gray. It will be a badge of honor in our marriage, visible proof of our longevity. Each of those silver hairs will be born and mature under my watch. I'm not sure if every wife feels this level of possession over them, but I do. Turning gray is a vulnerable moment, one that I have an exclusive front-row seat to. When we lie next to each other on the couch, I run my fingers across his scalp, exploring how coarse the silver are compared to the black. They curl more; Joe has always had such stick-straight hair, but now it's becoming a messy sea of dips and valleys. I love the transition.

"You teaching today?" I ask before I take a spoonful of cereal. I know the answer but like to let him think that I don't. Joe's first lecture is at eleven, his second at three thirty. He'll drive the half hour over to the clinic in between to check on his patients and do his rounds. Which means his patients will all see this side of him: his tailored suit pants, his crisp white button-up shirt, the cornflower-blue tie tightly knotted at his neck. He'll swap out the gray jacket for the white lab coat and likely hang a stethoscope around his neck, even though he rarely takes vitals. It's for the aesthetics, and aesthetics is something he's always done to perfection. It's one of the reasons I was drawn to and fell for him. Every detail of his life was in order. Crisp and clean. Compared to the turbulent madness of my family and upbringing, it was like crawling into a bed at a five-star hotel. A cocoon of safety and luxury.

That's how our marriage is. Perfect aesthetics.

It took me two years with Joe to understand what was necessary to maintain that level of peace and order. The sacrifices for the perfection.

I reach over and tap the top of the folder by his place at the table. "Don't forget that."

He picks it up and tucks it under his arm. "I'll see you tonight." He steps forward and kisses me on the top of the head, and he smells like his coconut shampoo and eucalyptus bodywash. "Love you."

"I love you too." I tilt back my chin, and he kisses me on the mouth, then gazes down at me for a moment, his eyes warm, his mouth in a slight smile.

The sacrifices are steep but worth it. For this man, I would do anything.

CHAPTER 19

DINAH

Yesterday, I didn't have a good chance to study the exterior of Reese Bishop's home, but this afternoon, the coroner and crime scene vans are gone, no black-and-whites cluttering the curb. Her street is the sort of Californian hodgepodge that occurs when flippers start creeping in. Half the houses are updated with new landscaping, pavered drives, and the sort of inexpensive updates that fool buyers into paying twice as much. The polished-up homes stand alongside overgrown lawns, shoddy architecture, and a few boarded-up places.

In the middle of the mayhem is Reese Bishop's house. It's a one-story ranch with a flat black roof, a yellow mailbox, and the impression that someone recently stopped trying. Maybe that's what happens when your heart stops showing up for work.

Yard care becomes unimportant.

Gutters overflow.

Trash bins don't always make it to the curb or back to their spot.

I park in Reese's driveway and use the emergency brake. After grabbing my bag, I ignore her front door and cross over to the adjacent house. It's 5:35 p.m., and her neighbor has a new Prius in the driveway, a bright-orange extension cord plugged into its back end.

I almost bought an electric car last year. Between my department-issued Lincoln and Joe's SUV, we didn't need a third vehicle, but I wanted something that would be good for the ranch and easy on our gas budget. I ordered a Subaru Outback hybrid with every bell and whistle. Two weeks later, I solved a murder investigation by tracking the suspect's activity using his car's Starlink system.

I canceled the Subaru the next day. It wasn't about being guilty of anything; it was about the unknown future. If there's ever a reason I don't want my actions to be known—either by the police, a government entity, or my spouse—the last thing I'll want is a vehicular tattletale.

Joe's SUV is a twenty-two-year-old Ford Excursion, a beast that guzzles gas, is impossible to park, and can transport a church choir without breaking a sweat or needing anyone to share a seat belt. It doesn't make financial, environmental, or common sense. I've brought up the idea of trading it in for something else, but he refuses, renting a car whenever he needs something more sensible or incognito.

Incognito is the last word I'd use to describe this neighbor's Prius, which is lime green with large daisy stickers all over it. There's no way the owner of this car has invested in security cameras, but I still press the doorbell and try. I smile when the woman answers the door, gesture toward Reese's house, ask the question, and try not to smile when she shakes her head.

I continue on, hitting the houses to the left, all the way up to the four-way stop at the entrance of her street.

I get nothing. There's not a single camera that faces the street or can provide helpful footage of who might have come and gone that Thursday.

I return to my car and sit in the driver's seat for a moment, unwrapping a chocolate-and-oatmeal protein bar and then taking a bite. It's one of the ones from Joe's clinic, and tastes like cardboard with a faintly medicinal aftertaste. There's still some ice water in my thermos tumbler, and I wash down the final bite. My blood sugar recovers, and I ball up the wrapper and tuck it into the pocket of my blazer. I open the door and head across the street, to the houses on the other side.

I hit pay dirt on the second one.

CHAPTER 20

JOE

After my class I drive a few miles out of my way and swing by my sister-in-law's work. I valet my SUV at the mall and walk a loop around the upper level of the center before taking a seat at one of the tables at the coffee shop across from the bakery. Marci is behind the pastry counter, her red apron on, her smile big as she helps a customer with their selection.

Marci is, to the traditional observer, the most attractive sister of the three. A pretty, polished garbage bag of a human. My wife has never said a negative thing about her younger sister, but I can feel the hostility between them. Marci tries, but Dinah is a brick wall covered with spikes, and I find the dynamic fascinating.

As a manager, Marci is sloppy. I watch as one of her employees leans against the wall, the girl's attention on her cell phone, her thumbs busy as she types out something on the screen. There's an empty plate still sitting on one of the tables, a crumpled napkin beside it, and a WET FLOOR sign that has been forgotten by a rack of merchandise.

I've asked Dinah about the emotional distance between her and Marci, and she says that they have never been close, but there is something else there. Sibling rivalries and strife are common in large families. But what is strange is that Dinah has stubbornly refused to discuss or acknowledge the origins of their estrangement. She thinks she's coy, that I don't suspect anything, but it's a stench that reeks from every interaction.

Every stiff hug.

Every carelessly chosen gift.

The lack of affection Dinah shows to Marci's children.

I've been coy myself. I don't ask too many questions, and I don't push hard. I act oblivious, but this is a mystery I will find the answer to. It's my favorite pastime, when I have time to think about it.

A man hovers by the edge of the counter, and Marci glances at him, then continues her conversation with a customer. I watch her closely, catching the widening of her smile, her stance suddenly straighter, her hands faster, the adjustment of her blouse and then her hair.

She likes him.

"May I help you?" A barista stops by my table, order pad in hand, and blocks my view.

"Americano," I mutter. "Large."

"Any cream or sugar?" she asks, shifting her weight onto one hip.

"No." I pull my seat closer to the table and try to see around her.

"I'll bring it out to you in a jiffy."

When she finally moves, Marci is standing at the end of the counter, talking to the man. He is smiling, his arms across his chest in an attempt to make himself look important. She laughs, reaching over to touch his shoulder, then brushes her fingers through her hair again.

I've considered killing this woman. I believe it would make my wife happy, but the unsurety of that outcome is why I haven't. It would be nice to detain Marci for a while and ask all the questions I want answers to.

I would enjoy opening up my sister-in-law's mind. She would crack quickly. In less than an hour, I estimate, her guts would spill all over the table.

I stand and open my billfold, withdrawing a twenty-dollar bill and leaving it on the table to cover my order. I don't need the coffee, or any more of Marci. It was interesting, her flirtation and possible affair—but that isn't why I've come.

I needed a fix, a deposit into the hobby that is my wife. This is a long-term study, one I'm in no hurry to complete. After all, once you know everything there is to know about a person, they lose their purpose.

Which is why, this weekend, I'll need to kill Melonie.

CHAPTER 21

DINAH

The woman's security footage is 4K and crystal clear, courtesy of a wired connection to the camera, which is set up beneath the home's eaves and well protected from wind, sun glare, and rain. My nose itches; somewhere in this house, there's got to be a cat.

"Okay, now, that's the day you're looking for, right there." The homeowner is a skinny Ukrainian woman with hoop earrings and a large mole on her cheek. She bends over my right shoulder, her long fingernail tapping on the tablet's screen. "You can watch it at four-times speed, but that's as fast as you can go. If you want to record anything, just use the—"

"I'm familiar with the software." I cut her off, hoping she'll take the hint and step back. She doesn't, and I clear my throat. "This could take me a while. Do you mind getting me some ice water? Or ideally, a tea or coffee?"

"Oh, sure." She pats my shoulder and scoots around the square dining table and into the galley kitchen. Alone with the tablet, I quickly skip to the time I need and watch the left corner of the screen, where half of Reese's driveway and her front door are visible. Three automobiles pass by, and the camera doesn't catch the tags but does clearly identify the vehicles. The second one causes my breath to hitch, and

I pause the video and zoom in on the driver's-side window. There's a reflection and I fast-forward, my back hunched, eyes tight on the screen. Ten minutes after the cars pass, one of the three returns. Eight minutes after that, the second.

I take photos of both cars with my phone, then fast-forward through the clip, scanning the street to see if there's a dog walker, a late-night jogger . . . anyone.

The street and sidewalk are empty. I glance toward the kitchen, then delete the clips. Going into the app settings, I locate the storage section and check the video-overwrite schedule. It is set to Never, so I quickly change it to a twenty-four-hour overwrite. By this time tomorrow, the entire day and the rest of the system's history will be gone.

"Anything?" The homeowner returns, a ceramic orange teacup in hand. On the front is a cat with a Cheshire grin. It's probably celebrating an allergy attack earned. As if on cue, my airways constrict further.

"Nothing." I tuck my phone into my pocket and rise to my feet. "But thank you for your time. Did you hear anything strange on Thursday morning? Anything out of the ordinary?"

"Nothing. What happened? Something with Reese?"

"We're trying to figure that out now. We don't have any evidence of foul play; we're just being diligent."

She nods, her expression grave. "Well, if I think of something, I'll call in and let you know. Here's the tea."

"I'm sorry, I just saw the time and have to run. But here's my card, if you think of something." I slide a business card from my wallet and hold it out to her. "My cell is on there. You can call anytime."

I let myself out and, once on the sidewalk, take a deep breath of air. Finally, the ability to breathe.

I finish my canvass, but all the other houses are duds.

CHAPTER 22

JESSICA

I bang on the room's locked door, but it's insulated with something. I slam my palm against it as hard as I can but don't produce enough sound to wake up a kitten. I do it for what feels like an hour, then stop.

I've tried screaming, so much so that my throat is hoarse and dry, and since there's no water in here, I've stopped that and am starting to have serious concerns about dehydration.

At some point, someone yelled at me to shut up. I think that's what they said. Whatever they yelled, I was in the middle of screaming when they did it, and I stopped and shouted, *"What?"* as loud as I could, but they didn't say anything else.

I'm certain there's some health department rule about me having access to drinking water. Hell, at the shelter, that's a requirement. Every dog has to have clean water available, all the time. And yet here I am. I've been in this room . . . what? Hours? Days? Not a water bottle in sight.

I pinch the skin on my forearm, and it easily pops back into place, so I guess I'm not too dehydrated. Not yet. But how long does it take to check on someone? Shouldn't they be doing rounds or something?

I can't believe I'm locked in this room with no bathroom, no shower, no water, no TV, no phone, no nurse's call button—nothing.

It's bullshit, and I'm going to write so many complaint letters . . . I'm going to drown this place in them. Google reviews, Yelp reviews, Facebook posts, Better Business Bureau . . . They are going to wish they'd never had me in here. I can be the biggest pain in the ass when I get fired up, and right now I have nothing to do but stew.

I sit on the bed and then lie back, letting out a slow breath as I think through my situation. This was not where I expected to be at this stage of my life: locked in a mental ward with greasy hair, adult diapers, and not a bit of technology. I would do a variety of filthy things right now for an iPhone with Candy Crush and internet access.

Maybe I did try to kill myself. At the rate this is going, I'll die from sheer boredom if the dehydration doesn't get me first.

CHAPTER 23

DINAH

"You think it's logical for a terminal patient to be suicidal?" I dip a crispy noodle into a small dish of sweet-and-sour sauce.

Joe considers the question as he chews on a mouthful of noodles. The Chinese takeout is stacked across our coffee table like mushrooms along a rotten piece of wood. There's shrimp fried rice, sweet-and-sour chicken, mu shu pork, and egg rolls, along with small bowls of Hunan, honey, and soy sauce.

We're sitting cross-legged on the floor beside the table, eating with chopsticks and our fingers, an old episode of *Cash Cab* running in the background. In between our conversation, we spit out answers to the contestants' queries. We rarely lose a question, and are united in our opinion that, if given the choice to double-or-nothing our prize money on a bonus question, we'd risk it all in a heartbeat.

Joe takes a sip of tea, then wipes his mouth with a monogrammed paper napkin. It has *J & D* on the front in expensive calligraphy font. He thinks they are left over from our wedding, but the truth is that I order them by the case and continually restock the pantry when we get low. I like the subconscious reminder it gives him of our wedding day, which was a seamless execution of romance, made possible by multiple wedding planners and a six-figure budget. We had two hundred guests and a six-course reception dinner. Afterward, we flew first class to Tahiti, and it was there, floating on a raft in an emerald-green lagoon, where I admitted to him that my insecurity was what had fueled every decision in the wedding-planning. The event ended up being a personal statement, one I had underlined with personal caviar boats and a twelve-member orchestra: *Look, I am worthy of being loved.*

He kissed me deeply and told me that I never had to worry about being loved again. That he would love me through the good and the bad, the beautiful moments and the ugly ones.

He told me that, in a black-and-white world of women, I stood out in full color.

That I fascinated him.

That he was wholly and entirely addicted to me.

"You are not just worthy of being loved," he said thickly, the water glinting with a thousand shimmers from the sun. "You are designed for it, and I was designed to fulfill that honor."

It wasn't possible for me to fall further in love with him, but what did happen in that moment was that I fell a little bit in love with myself. And for a woman who had hated herself for over a decade, that meant everything.

Joe clears his throat, and it takes me a moment to remember that I asked him about the likelihood of a terminally ill patient being suicidal.

"It depends on the individual. For some, absolutely. For others, extremely unlikely."

"I'd do it," I state, dunking my egg roll in some of the pink sauce. "I'd take myself out before I made you suffer through my final months."

"Yeah, but you're not a mother," he says, and the swiftness of the response deepens the stab.

"What difference does that make?" I stuff the egg roll into my mouth and hope it hides my frown.

You aren't a mother. Had he sounded accusatory, or was I just sensitive?

"A mother wouldn't be thinking about herself or their spouse; she's going to be in the mindset of thinking about her children. That's all she's going to be thinking of. Preparing them for what is to come. Sharing all of her wisdom with them. Telling them everything she thinks they might ever need to know. Of course, I'm referring to young children. Someone, say, your mom's age . . . with mature children?" He shrugs. "The connection and concern weaken with age. I've talked to you in the past about how dynamic system approaches organize behavior around coherent patterns of interaction . . ." He pauses, waiting for confirmation.

"Yeah." I nod as if I know what he's talking about and hope he doesn't reopen the lecture. *The connection weakens with age.* Jessica Bishop is twenty years old. How strong would her desire be for a connection with her mother? What kind of bond did she have with Reese? Maybe Reese started spilling secrets in her final days.

Joe is rambling about how adaptive relationships can flexibly reorganize as adolescents enter adulthood, and I interrupt him to point out a *Cash Cab* question about Formula 1, a topic he loves just as much as behavioral theory.

You aren't a mother.

There had been something there. An edge. A bite. And that is ridiculous, because just like our tastes in music and films and food and love, we're in sync with our opinions on children. Have been from the start.

Our relationship is a two-person union. Any addition to that will only detract from our life.

CHAPTER 24

JESSICA

I'm asleep when the doctor returns. When I wake up, he's sitting on the edge of my bed, watching me. I blink and rub the dried crust away from the corners of my eyes.

He's got kind of a Bradley Cooper vibe. I guarantee you, Mom's gonna flip when she meets him, then try to set us up, despite the fact that he's got to be a decade older than me. She's always said I should date a doctor, though I'm not sure she meant a shrink. Are they even real doctors? Maybe this guy just likes dressing up in a lab coat.

"Hi." He smiles, and I realize we've just been sitting here staring at each other for a few minutes now. Normally, that would bother me, but everything feels very chill, and I realize I must be high. Maybe not high—drugged. Definitely floating on something.

"Hi." I lift my hand, and the IV has been reattached. I follow the line to a pouch of liquids, hanging from a stand by the bed. Oh, that's right. A nurse came to my room at some point and gave me water and some pills. She stayed with me for a bit and helped me into bed. I asked her lots of questions. What were they?

"How are you feeling?" he asks.

"Okay. Foggy."

"Do you remember your name?"

My name. I shake my head, and my hair falls in front of my eyes. I start to move it and remember two things in rapid succession:

First, I still haven't had a shower.

Second, I tried to slit my wrists.

"I need a shower." I tuck my hair behind my ear and turn my hand over, looking at the bandage. It looks new, and I wonder if I did it or the nurse did.

"You'll need assistance to do that. You're too much of a risk right now to shower unattended. Do you want me to take you to the shower now?"

I frown, trying to process the idea of what him taking me to the shower means. "You would walk me there?"

"I would have to go in with you. It's fine if you aren't comfortable with that. We can wait until the nurse is back, but it might be a little bit."

"I'll wait." My head itches, and I scratch my scalp. I didn't think it was possible to get more greasy, but it is. As badly as I need a shower, the idea of him going in with me seems weird. Super weird.

"What's with the bandages on my wrists?" I hold them out to show him.

"You came in with some injuries. Have you tried to hurt yourself in the past?"

Hurt myself? I shake my head. "No."

"Are you sure?" He smiles as if he knows something I don't. "Maybe you wouldn't remember."

Well, he has me there. Given that I can't remember my name or any major pieces of my backstory, it's entirely possible I was trying to off myself on a weekly basis—but why? What about my life is so horrible?

I don't remember it being horrible. Other than Mom being sick, it's pretty good.

"Do you remember why you admitted yourself?" His voice is kinder now; there's an apology in his tone.

"No." I hate this game. "Why?"

"I'd really like for you to remember it, if you can."

"I don't. I've tried. You locked me in here for like two days with literally nothing to do but think. I can't remember anything."

"It wasn't two days, but I understand how time can get lost in a place like this. We can do our next session in my office, if you'd prefer a change of location."

"How about I go home and then come back on another day, and then we can do it in your office then?"

He pauses. "You want to leave here?"

I let out a laugh. "Uh, yeah. Do most people like being here?"

"We're the highest-rated facility in the county, if not the state. Trust me when I say that there are a lot worse places you can be."

"It's just that I'm going crazy in here." I wince. "Sorry. That's probably offensive to the other patients."

"Because you don't belong here—is that how you feel? That the other patients are 'crazy' and you aren't?" He puts the word in quotes. He's still smiling, but I feel like he's getting offended by this. "I'll bring in some books and puzzles. Things to keep you entertained."

"I'm *not* crazy, if that's what you're implying." I may not know my name, but I know that whatever happened the other night . . . it was a fluke. A bad trip on whatever drug I took. Nothing else.

"Would it surprise you to find out that you are the highest-risk patient in this facility?"

"Yeah," I scoff. "Yeah, that would surprise me."

He stands up, and I wonder if it's too late to change my mind about taking a shower. "You aren't able to leave our facility because you're on a 5150 hold. It's a three-day hold, but one that we can extend for up to fourteen days if there's continued concern. Given what you told us when you were admitted, we've already extended the time frame. You're going to be with us for at least two more weeks, if not longer. You are not special or above any other patient in this facility."

"Fourteen days?" I stare at him. "I can't be here that long. I have . . ." I don't know what I have, but I feel like there is a job.

Something with a guy named Rick. No, Rob. Finally, someone's name. "I have a job."

"Good. Tell me about it." He pulls a pen from the pocket of his lab coat and clicks it. "Where do you work?"

This feels like a challenge, and unfortunately, I'm going to fail it.

He waits, his brow raised, and I grind my teeth together and remember that I have a night guard that I'm supposed to wear when I sleep. Another useless item that won't get me out of here.

"Well?" he prods. "Where do you work?"

"I don't know." I push off the bed and onto my feet.

"I had hoped that you would regain some of your memory naturally, but maybe it would help if I told you what you shared with us on the night you were admitted."

"You think?" I throw up my hands, and the IV pulls in a painful fashion. I move closer to its stand.

He pauses, and I don't know why he can't just spit it out. "Well, you were upset and bleeding." He nods at my wrists. "You said you wanted to kill yourself."

"That doesn't make sense," I argue.

He holds up a hand. "Please, let me continue, because we get a lot of suicidal visitors here. It was *why* you were suicidal that caused the extended 5150 hold."

If there was a way to pull words out of someone's throat, I would. I knot my hands together and force myself to keep my mouth shut so he will finish.

He meets my eyes, and the cocky look from earlier is gone. Now he looks somber and a little sad, and the combination is alarming.

"You also told us that you had just killed your mother."

It's no longer a struggle to keep my mouth closed.

That bit of information renders me speechless.

CHAPTER 25

DINAH

Freddie is waiting at the Beverly Hills station when I walk in, Styrofoam coffee cup in hand. I eye him as I climb the steps to the entrance turnstiles. I pull out my key card and swipe it, and am buzzed in. "He's with me," I say to Olga, who nods and flashes Freddie a big smile.

"What are you doing here?" I push through the second interior door and into the stairwell.

"Wanted to talk about the case," he says, jogging up the stairs as if they weren't built at a ridiculous angle guaranteed to suck the life out of your chest. "APB turned up Jessica Bishop's car."

"Where?" At the second stairwell landing is a framed photo of Oley. I touch it out of habit as I round the turn and head up the final flight of steps.

"LAX, long-term parking."

"Okay. You check flights?"

"Yeah, there was already a flag on that. No flights."

"You check the bus terminal there?"

"Yep. Same." He holds open the door to the hall, and I take it, weaving through the maze until I come to my office door.

Pulling my keys lanyard off my neck, I unlock the office door. "Maybe she got an Uber from there. Took it to the border."

"Or maybe her kidnapper ditched it there, and—" He pauses in the doorway. "Damn, Marino. Nice digs."

"It's an office," I say dryly, but part of my chest puffs up at his reaction. Joe hired an interior designer to outfit the space. While everyone else has cheap desks and stacks of files and boxes everywhere, I have a custom-built credenza that takes up the entire back wall. It has a fish tank, a section for manuals and books, hidden file drawers, a mini-fridge, and a large whiteboard and bulletin board. My desk's surface is spotless, with a wireless lamp on one corner and a pen caddy on the other. There is one leather chair in the corner for guests, though I rarely have any. "Sit." I point to the chair. "You still think she was kidnapped?"

"There're six lots at LAX. She picked the one lot that doesn't have a camera at the ticket gate and parked on the far end, out of views of the spotlight cams."

"So she's at the north end." I sink into my chair and drop my purse on the floor. "I agree: not ideal."

"I did an inventory of cars at the north end, from oldest to newest. Want to take a guess at how many belong to missing women?"

My stomach clenches. "Not really."

"Fourteen."

"Are you thinking sex trafficking?"

"Or a serial killer."

I drop my head back and laugh. "Come on, Freddie. We just wrapped up the Bloody Heart Killer."

"A city can have two serial killers at the same time."

"How long ago is the oldest missing woman?"

"Six years ago."

"Damn, how rarely does that lot tow?" I don't like the look in his eye. It's fiery, like how Oley used to get when he saw the Krispy Kreme "Hot Now" sign lit up. A man on a mission. Why couldn't I have gotten a trainee who was skating through on the bare minimum and asking about law enforcement discounts? Instead, I have someone imagining up a serial killer and doing audits on airport parking lots.

"Well?" He rubs his palms together like he's really onto something. "What do you think?"

"Define *missing*."

"What?"

"You said that there are the cars of fourteen missing women in that lot. I'm curious if we're talking runaway teens or dental hygienists in happy marriages who've suddenly disappeared."

"Well, I haven't had time to dig into all of them yet—"

"How many pretty girls under twenty-five?" I interrupt.

"I don't know," he hedges, and I'm pretty sure he knows exactly how many there are.

"Guess," I order.

"Nine or ten."

I roll my eyes. "It's sex trafficking, Freddie. Come on. You know it is."

"No, I think it's more than this. Jessica is too clean. No evidence at the house—not a scrap of it. Her phone's dropped off the grid. No pings, no digital trail, no activity. Her car gets left in one of the only places in town where it won't be noticed or flagged for a ticket or towing, and no cameras." He stands, and I don't like the agitation, the way he runs his hands through his dark hair and pulls at the strands. He's in training. His second or third month. This is his first missing woman, who might not even be missing. He'll have to toughen up or else he'll never survive.

I think of Blythe Howard, my first missing woman, who hadn't been missing—not at first. Her baby had been found in a library parking lot's trash bin. The tiny infant had ligature marks around her neck that the coroner's office believed were made by an extension cord.

I had a meltdown over the case. My detective's badge was barely out of the wrapper, and the DA was refusing to press any charges against Blythe, citing insufficient evidence. I became obsessed with the crime scene, the mother's background, the autopsy details . . . I started neglecting my other cases, my relationships; everything fell to the side in my outrage at the crime against this helpless baby.

My lieutenant had referred me to the staff psychologist, who was also fairly green in his field. I rapped my knuckles against the shrink's eighth-floor-office door, bristling with indignation and ready to snap off his head at the first indication that there was anything wrong with caring about a murdered infant.

Then Joe opened the door and smiled, and I knew, right there in that moment, that he would make everything okay. That he would be different from every other man I'd ever known. That he would listen and not judge. That he would take care of me.

And he did. He wrapped his words around me like a warm blanket, one that held me to his chest and rubbed my back and whispered in my ear that everything was going to be okay.

And eventually, it was, though Blythe was never prosecuted, and ran off in the middle of the night a week before I finally got a warrant for her arrest.

Too bad Freddie won't experience the same level of treatment for his new-detective neuroticism. His psych eval will be with Joe's replacement, a chain-smoking New Yorker who constantly invites me to join her bocce ball team. I visited her once for a mandatory eval after I discharged my weapon at a scene. It was a complete waste of an hour of both my time and hers.

I refocus on Freddie. He's standing in front of my fish tank, staring at Pickles the eel, who's gaping at him in hopes that he'll drop a pellet into the water.

"Listen to yourself. Sometimes the scene is clean because there is no scene." I spin in my chair so that I'm facing him and tick off the reasons on my fingers. "No bruising on Reese Bishop's neck or body. No needle marks. No one was forcing poison down her throat. No foreign fingerprints on her coffee cup or in the kitchen. No disturbances in the neighborhood, and the neighbors didn't see anything strange. No sign of a struggle in the home or in the daughter's bedroom. There's literally nothing suspicious about this, Freddie. No offense, but I have other cases to deal with."

"I talked to my TO about it," he says stubbornly.

"Good for you. So glad you interrupted Ron's hospital stay for this. What'd he say?"

"He said to check the time stamps. See what time the daughter's car got to the airport. Cross-reference that with the ME's time of death."

Not a bad suggestion. I pick up my phone and scroll through the digital file, clicking on the autopsy report. Time of death is listed between 6:00 a.m. and noon on Tuesday. A wide-ass range, if any hypothesis is going to be made based on Jessica Bishop's travel. Still, I ask, "When was Jessica's car left at the airport?"

"7:15 a.m."

"It tracks. Also tracks with her killing her mom, waking up, and finding her dead and freaking out . . . really any of our proposed scenarios, with the exception of her being on vacation in Tijuana and oblivious to all of this." I place my phone on the desk. "I don't know what that solves."

"Well, it gives us a better idea of her movements." He hunches his shoulders forward as he tucks both hands in his pockets. "Aren't you worried about her? Think of it like she was your daughter."

"Oh, don't give me that shit. It's a big city, Freddie. Do you know how many lost women we have right now? Do you?" I raise my brows.

"A lot."

"Over four hundred. Is her phone still on the move?"

He shakes his head, and if there is a way for a human to deflate, he's doing it now. "No, it's disappeared. But I'm telling you, Dinah, this is a professional. He knows how to kill a phone, how to hide his tracks."

"Suspicions aren't enough in this business," I say a little more gently. "You have to pick and choose what you bring to the DA. You bring them shit, they're going to remember that and be tougher on your next one." I think of the baby, of my impassioned plea to the DA to arrest Blythe Howard. "Trust me. There's not enough here. But you did good legwork on this. Great job."

He scowls and slouches back in the seat. "How is it a great job? You think Jessica thinks we're doing a great job?"

I stand and grab my keys. "Come on. Let's take a field trip. I want to show you something."

CHAPTER 26

DINAH

I told Freddie there are four hundred missing women in Los Angeles, but the exact number fluctuates at any given moment between three hundred and five hundred. Unfortunately, most are never found. I know the stats better than anyone; missing persons was my world for three years before I moved into homicide, and it almost killed me.

If it hadn't been for Joe, I wouldn't have made it through. He taught me how to disassociate; how to compartmentalize my emotions and leave my work in the station, in the squad car, in the crime scene. Now when I step out of the station or into our home, I don't think about dead bodies or tearful parents. I enter our cocoon and his arms, and a switch flips in my mind and I become Dinah: loving wife.

Dinah, who spends four hours on her homemade cinnamon rolls.

Dinah, who irons Joe's shirts with extra starch and puts peppermints in his pockets.

Dinah, who helps him at the clinic and scrubs urine off walls and makes care packages for patients at Christmas and who gets screamed at and spat at but never once thanked.

That Dinah can't coexist with Detective Marino, who's investigating the father who handcuffed his son to a bed and lit him on fire. Detective Marino, who promised a grieving mother four years ago that she'd find her daughter's killer and didn't. Detective Marino, who wakes up in the middle of the night with nightmares of gruesome crime scenes.

Joe didn't marry a detective. My mother didn't birth a detective. My nieces and nephews don't run into the arms of a detective. Compartmentalization is the key to mental survival—but I'm not here to teach Freddie that. I'm here to show him this board and all the missing women with their own stories and validations and reasons why they desire our time and attention.

I walk down the length of the board, and my gaze instinctively finds the names and faces etched in my mind.

Gabriella Montleigh. An ex-cheerleader who liked reggae music, her pet pug, and a little cocaine on the weekends. Never found.

Tricia Higgins. Mother of two with crippling PTSD from two tours in Iraq. Never found.

Riley Biff. Diner waitress who liked older men, preferably married. Never found.

Lacey Deltour.

Melonie Piat.

Blythe Howard.

My gaze finds and sticks on the image of Blythe, her photo high up on the wall. In the photo, her face is full, her expression somber. It's a candid shot, taken when she was pregnant.

Looking at this wall is like walking through a graveyard of all the cases I've worked. All still missing.

"This one says Beverly Hills," Freddie says, looking at a blonde in the upper corner, and I know without stepping closer that he's looking at Riley Biff. A collage of images shutters through in my mind—the blond track star, her mom tearfully begging for leads, the hundreds of high school students holding candles at her memorial.

Unlike some of the others, Riley wasn't a troubled teen who had run away or an abused wife looking for a clean start. Her absence was a highly publicized event, one I learned a lot from.

He reads out her name, then glances at me. "I think I remember this one."

"It was everywhere." I join him and stare at the flyer, forcing my features to remain calm and fixed. No emotion. No sign of how the girl's photo affects me. "But you would have been young . . . I'm surprised you remember it."

He laughs. "Not that young. I was . . ." He leans forward and reads the date on the flyer. "Twenty-two. Only six years ago."

Six years ago. It feels like twenty. I watch as he rests his forearm against the wall, his face two feet from the flyer, reading every detail, and wonder why he picked this flyer out of all of them. Am I just that unlucky? Or is this something else? A dig? Did Thompson tell him about my history, of the different girls I never found?

"Disappeared right before prom," he reads off the page. "What high school did she go to?"

"Good Shepherd."

He looks up, thinking. "I don't know that one."

"It's Catholic." I cross my arms over my chest. "My niece went there. She's a year younger than Riley."

"Oh, that's interesting." It feels like an accusation, and I get the sense that he already knew about my connection to Riley and the case. Sophie didn't even know Riley—not in any way other than how a victim knows her bullies and an unpopular girl knows the queens.

Then again, maybe I'm being paranoid. I always am, in this building. I've worked too hard to earn this shield, my office, my caseload, and reputation.

"You know, this board doesn't help me care any less about Jessica," Freddie says flatly, stepping back and looking over the wall, which stretches from the data bullpen all the way down to the restrooms. "We need to get better. Dig deeper. You think you're discouraging me, but you aren't. You're just making me want to work harder."

"Good." I pat his arm, then squeeze it. "I'm glad you got fire, Freddie. I just don't want you to waste it on a case that won't go anywhere. If you're itching to work on something, find some of these. Read these summaries. Find the low-hanging fruit. Bring them home to their families."

He nods somberly, like my advice is hitting home, but I know the look in his eyes. I recognize it.

He's a tick and he's stuck to this case. Stuck to Jessica. Stuck to Reese. Stuck to me.

I drop my hand from his arm, breaking the connection.

CHAPTER 27

JESSICA

I am lost at everything he told me.

The evidence is clear. The cuts are on my wrists. I believe him when he says I told him I killed my mom. If there was anything that would have led me to a suicide attempt and committing myself to a mental institution, killing her would have triggered that.

But I don't have the capacity to do that. I wouldn't have. I *loved* my mom. Like, more than any other daughter on the planet. I would never have hurt her.

Though, if I did . . . I look down at the bandages again. Yeah. Slitting my wrists and driving to a mental institution . . . it tracks.

My memories of the last twenty-four hours before coming here are spotty, but the ones that I do have don't show any triggers or foreshadowing of a murderous rampage on my part.

I need to get off this medicine. Whatever they're giving me is making it impossible to cut through the fog, though maybe that's the purpose. The doc gave me another IV before he left—said it was for nutrients and fluids, and I'm already beginning to nod off, my alarm at his information mellowing into an almost casual acceptance of the fact.

I killed my mother—that's what he said. I killed my mother and tried to kill myself.

I lie back down on the bed and curl onto one side, looking at the white wall. Sometimes my mom gets in bed with me. She curls up behind me and traces her finger along the muscles in my back and tells me how, when I was a baby, I would fall asleep with my hand grasping her finger.

She always falls asleep before me and snores like a broken chain saw, with lots of sputters and starts.

It doesn't make sense. I love my mom.

CHAPTER 28

DINAH

I hate Marci. Right now, she's leaning over her husband's shoulder, looking at his cards, her claws digging into his neck. She's giggling, and when her gaze darts my way, I look down at my cards. My spite is a pill I've hidden for two decades, and her ignorance of it is one of the only things that makes it bearable. I won't ever give her the satisfaction of knowing how much I care.

No one loved me back then. No one, but maybe he had been close. Close and then gone, in love with her, and I had to lie in my bed each night and listen to her giggle to him on the phone.

Sal pushes a stack of blue poker chips forward, and Eric follows suit. I glance at Eric, and our eyes meet. His mouth curves. It would serve her right if I returned the favor and let her see how betrayal felt. It is painful, yes—but from your own sister? Horrible.

"You got what it takes, Dinah?" He winks at me. He really is a terrible husband. Joe would never wink at another woman. His gaze wouldn't drop to her neckline, which is where Eric's has just fallen. Joe wouldn't make it obvious, every chance he got, that he would take his wife's sister upstairs and fuck her until he collapsed.

That's exactly what Eric does. I could have screwed my sister's husband a hundred times since they've been together, but I haven't. I wouldn't, even if she does deserve it—even if the thought of the revenge is delicious.

Four hundred missing women in this city, yet she couldn't be one of them. I tuck my cards under the stack and push a pile of red chips toward the middle. "Raise."

CHAPTER 29

DINAH

Chunky Mike's is an ice-cream shop in a strip mall with a barbershop, bookstore, shoe-repair shop, and mini-mart. The trash can outside Chunky Mike's is overflowing, and there's a transient sleeping on the bench two storefronts down. I park in front of the store and eye the subject as we step out.

The guy doesn't budge, and I grimace at the sight of Freddie, who opens the glass entrance door with a dramatic sweeping motion of his arm.

"Stop," I warn.

"Think that was bad, wait until I buy you a sundae," he drawls. "Sprinkles and everything."

I ignore him and approach the counter, where a yellow-smocked teenager looks up with a smile. "Hello, how can I help you?"

"We have a few questions about one of your employees." I pull out my business card and pass it to her. "We're with LAPD. I'm Detective Marino and this is Freddie. He's in training; you can ignore him."

"Ouch," Freddie mutters. "Should I sit at the kiddie table outside?"

The dark-haired girl studies the card, then looks back at me. Tapping the card on the top of the register, she pauses before brightening. "Cookies and cream with chocolate hardshell in a waffle cone, right?"

"Excuse me?" Freddie asks.

"That's her order." She nods toward me. "Right?"

"Uh, no." I shake my head with a firm glare and will the woman to take the hint.

She doesn't. "No, that's it. I never forget a face or an order. Just takes me a couple seconds sometimes." She laughs. "But you weren't all dressed up last time."

Freddie chuckles, his gaze dropping to my rumpled suit. "Dressed up?" he says under his breath.

"I'm a plain-vanilla girl," I say crisply. "One scoop in a cup is fine."

"Oh, come on. It was like three weeks ago, right?"

Three weeks ago on the nose. She could be an expert witness.

"I was just about to go on vacation," she continues. "You were asking us about the—"

"Okay, fine," I interrupt. Jesus, someone needs to slice this girl's lips off. What kind of ice-cream scooper has a photographic memory? "I'll take cookies and cream. Sounds good."

Freddie is studying me, and this is what I get for letting him tag along. I should have just come here alone—asked my questions, satisfied my curiosity, and left. Instead, I felt some ridiculous urge to prove to him that I was doing my job and following any leads, and crossing *questioning friends and coworkers* off the investigative to-do list.

So I visited an ice-cream shop last month. Who cares?

"Coming right up." She beams and turns to Freddie. "And you?"

"Mint chocolate chip. Three scoops, please. I'll take a waffle cone as well." He leans his weight on the counter and looks around. "Just you working?"

"Yep. Mornings are slow. We have two on in the afternoon. You here to ask about Jessica?"

"We are." I withdraw the thin leather sleeve where I keep my driver's license and a credit card.

"I figured so. We've all been talking. You know, I'm covering her shift right now. We knew as soon as she no-showed on Tuesday that something was wrong. I mean, she's like our best employee. Always here early."

"What kind of girl is she?" I ask. "Partier? Catty? Quiet?"

"Ummm . . ." She takes her time scooping out my ice cream, her forehead wrinkling in concentration. "I wouldn't say she's a partier, but she was open to stuff—if you know what I mean."

"No, we don't know what you mean," I say.

"Well, I never went out with her, but I do know that she went out. She would be kinda hungover sometimes. She was always going to clubs in Hollywood. She went on a date once with Trent Iverson, you know. Before he died. She talked about that a lot. I don't know that it was a *date* as much as like a hookup at a party, but still . . ." She laughs and turns a container of chocolate syrup upside down, drizzling it over my ice cream.

"Did she ever mention her mom?" The abruptness of Freddie's question rubs me the wrong way, and I force myself to put my credit card on the top of the register and keep my mouth shut.

"Oh yeah, all the time. The last few months, we've shifted the schedule a lot for her so she can take her mom to appointments." She lowers her voice. "You know, her mom is like, dying. It's really bad."

"Is that what Jessica told you? That she's dying?" Freddie asks.

"Well, no. She was always optimistic about it. But Jeff—he works the afternoon shift—his aunt had the same thing that her mom has, and his aunt wasn't as bad as her mom, and his aunt died, so we all kind of understand what's up." She looks at Freddie, then me. "Who's taking her to her appointments, with Jessica missing? I can if she needs me to."

"I think it's taken care of," I say quickly before Freddie opens his big mouth. "Did Jessica seem to like her mom? They got along well?"

"Oh, they are best friends. Her mom is like, the coolest. Especially for an older mom. She brought all of us lemon squares for Christmas in these little tins that were decorated with our name on the front. I have a picture of mine if you want to see it. I posted it on Insta." She passes Freddie his green-and-black tower of scoops, and there's zero chance he'll be able to eat it without making a mess of his dress shirt.

I take a bite out of mine and wait for her to ring us up. "Any other close friends you're aware of? We're making the rounds, trying to paint a picture of her life."

"Well, Kristy. She's a super-tall Black girl, really pretty. Gets a scoop of strawberry and a Gatorade. And she was dating some guy who drove a Corvette. Kinda shaggy hair. I don't know what his name was; she always acted like it wasn't serious. But he got a root beer float when he came in." She taps the register's screen with slow movements, like it's her first time using it.

"Anything seem odd with her in the last month? Any phone calls that upset her . . . or missed shifts . . . new behavior. Anything like that?" I already know what she's going to say. This is a dead end, with expensive sprinkles on top.

"No. Maybe a little sad and stressed about her mom, but it's been like that for the last few months, ever since her diagnosis."

Yes, she loved her mom. Daughter of the Year. We got it.

"She have a temper?" Freddie asks suddenly, and I glance at him as I sign the receipt, giving her a hefty tip.

She frowns, thinking over the question. "No, not that I ever saw. But this is like, the best job ever." She spreads her arms out to encompass the tiny shop. "I mean, like, what's there to be mad about?"

Oh, to be this young and dumb. I smile at her. "Good point. Thanks a lot . . . What was your name?"

"Claire. Claire Brender."

"Thanks, Claire." I raise my cone in parting and try to ignore the dribble of melted ice cream running down my fingers. "Call us if you think of anything."

Freddie holds open the door for me and gestures to one of the two small tables under the building's eaves. "Shall we?"

I hesitate, glancing toward my car, but the last thing I need is ice cream on my seats. "Yeah," I say reluctantly, and take the metal seat he holds out for me.

CHAPTER 30

DINAH

"So, you've been here before?" Freddie jumps on the topic the moment my butt hits the wobbly metal chair.

"I guess so?" I say dubiously. "I mean, I do like cookies and cream at times." I glance toward the shop. "I wouldn't put my memory against hers. Talk about a steel trap." I nibble on the top of my cone.

"Yeah, she'd be great in a police lineup. How come we never get anyone like that?"

I snort. "Oh yes. In your vast years of experience, right?"

"Hey, am I wrong?" He puffs out his chest and has the nerve to look offended.

"You aren't totally wrong." I shrug and watch as a pigeon pecks at a piece of gum that's stuck to the pavement.

"What do you think is up with Jessica? I mean, really." He takes a giant bite of his ice cream and smacks his way through it, opening his mouth way more than necessary.

I think she's going to die. I hide the thought in a bite of waffle cone, and take my time chewing before I answer. "I don't think she murdered Reese. I think she found her and freaked out and ran."

"Why don't you think she killed her?"

Telling him the truth—that I didn't need him to have any more interest in this case than he already did—probably wouldn't fly. "Look, Freddie, I know you really want this to be a murder, but like I told you before, wanting something and it being true are two different things. Jessica is, by all accounts, a sane, well-adjusted young woman, with no criminal priors, no history of violence, no motive . . . So it doesn't fit."

"No motive except for the life insurance policy." He wiggles his eyebrows at me. If I had a knife, I would carve them off his face.

"We checked for a life insurance policy," I counter.

"We checked national databases, but not the secondary market." He gives me a smug smile, and the last thing I need is a damn life insurance policy showing up.

I close my eyes, annoyed with myself for not digging deeper and finding this out. "How much is it?"

"Fifty thousand dollars."

Fifty thousand dollars. For Joe and me, it'd be nothing. A drop in the bucket. But for so many individuals, it was life changing and worth killing for. I've found murderers who had extinguished a life for as little as five or ten thousand bucks. I've found even more who've done it for free.

This is something that could cause a judge to pay attention, and that is the opposite of what I need. "Jessica is the beneficiary? Any trust or stipulations on the inheritance?"

"Sole beneficiary, and nope—fifty K, straight to her upon signature of a death certificate."

"Have you called them to see if she has contacted them?"

He pauses. "No. Haven't gotten that far."

He hasn't *thought* that far. There's a difference, but I let it slide. "You read the policy? There's no exclusion for suicide or potential foul play?"

His enthusiasm wanes further. "No, I didn't."

"Who's the insurance policy through?"

"Winwood United Securities."

I think, then shake my head. "Never heard of them. I'll have to request a copy of the policy and talk to the agent they assign to her case." A car beside mine shifts into reverse and creeps out of the space, then turns to the left and heads slowly out of the parking lot. I don't like its pace, and I stare at the back of the car, committing the license plate—56K2D—to memory. 56K2D. Maybe nothing, but maybe something. Every detail is innocent until it is guilty. People are often the inverse—everyone is guilty until they are innocent, at least in my eyes.

Take Freddie. We've been together almost forty-five minutes now, but this is the first he's mentioned of the insurance policy. The only real evidence to support his obsession with Reese's supposed murder, and he doesn't mention it until now. Why? It's suspicious, and I fucking hate suspicious behavior outside one of my cases.

"Why did you sit on this?" I set my cone down on the table between us because there's no way I'm lollipop-licking my way through it in front of him, not while I have a ring on my finger and a shred of dignity left. "Why not tell me the moment you discovered it?"

"I guess I wanted to see if you would find it."

"You wanted to see if I would find it?" I narrow my eyes. "This isn't a cop-off, Freddie. It's a murder investigation."

"Well, that's the first I've heard you call it that. Let me correct what I said earlier: I wasn't waiting to see if you would find it; I waited to see if you'd look for it."

I let out a strangled laugh. "I'm sorry, who died to have you testing me? You're lucky I let you tag along on this errand."

"Reese Bishop died." He leans forward and levels me with a look that I don't like at all. "And Jessica Bishop isn't the only girl who is missing on your watch. Lacey Deltour. Blythe Howard. Riley Biff. I could name a half dozen more if you want me to."

Not a half dozen more. *Four* more. And he doesn't have to name them, because their names are tattooed on my brain. I swallow, but my throat is sticky with sweet.

"I'm not a trainee, Dinah. I'm with IA."

IA. Internal Affairs. I don't understand it yet I do, all at once. I clear my throat. "I'm under investigation?"

No fucking wonder he's been up my ass. Part of me thought it was a crush, had worried about Joe's reaction, but this is so much worse. I think of my visit to the neighbors. The deleted video. Does he know about that? Is there a tracker on my car? How long have I been watched—and how, in all the ineptitude of the LAPD, did I come to be on anyone's radar?

"I wouldn't call it an 'investigation'; I'd call it concern from up top. You're sloppy, Dinah."

Sloppy. I take a deep breath. "Just because I missed the life insurance policy doesn't mean that I haven't— I mean, that was just one thing."

He stands and has the audacity to take another bite of his cone, crunching through the waffle tip like he's a six-year-old. I remember his pause at the missing person's board, his fixation on Riley Biff. I should have trusted my gut. "I've been one step ahead of you the entire time. I've been feeding you clues and watching you intentionally ignore them."

"You've been all over the board," I shot back. "You think Jessica's a victim of a serial killer, then you think she killed her mom for life insurance. Pick a damn theory. Oh, wait, you can't, because there isn't enough for any of them to stick!" I rise to my feet in an attempt to be on his level. "Screw you, Freddie. Want to write a report to IA? Go ahead. I'm the best fucking detective Beverly Hills has. Look at my record. Do I have unsolves? Sure. Missing persons? Who doesn't? You want to pick apart my old cases, go ahead—but I'm not wrong on this one. Reese Bishop killed herself. Jessica Bishop isn't being held by a serial killer, and didn't poison her mom and take off for Mexico. All that is bullshit theories and will get you laughed out of the DA's office."

I grab my keys off the table and pick up my ice-cream cone, which is now a mess of melted chocolate and cream. Swearing, I drop it into the trash can and wipe off my hands with the napkin, then throw it in after the cone.

"Wait, Dinah." He stays in step with me, and I use my key to manually open my door, making sure the passenger side stays locked.

"Get your own ride back." I get in and close the door on him. He raps on my window, but I ignore him, hitting the lock button.

I start the engine, inhale deeply, and try to center myself as best I can, despite the increased staccato of his knuckles on the window.

You're sloppy. Is that what they think? That's their focus? Incompetence versus guilt? I put the car in reverse and stomp on the gas, praying that I run over his foot in the process. I kiss my fingers, tap Oley's whistle, and send a quick apology to the man upstairs. Whipping the car out and forward, I gun it for the exit and leave Freddie behind, his hands up in the air, frustration all over his handsome face.

Fuck. Fuck. Fuck. Fuckity-fuck.

CHAPTER 31

DINAH

Joe can absolutely not find out about the IA investigation.

I drive faster than I should, weaving in and out of traffic on the 110. The issue is with Freddie as much as it is with the investigation. I should have told Joe about him the minute he showed up at Reese Bishop's crime scene. But I didn't. I go through that day, and the next, and the next. I met him in my office. I hid in my mother's house and spoke to him on the phone. I went to Baby's Coffee with him. I drove him to get ice cream, for fuck's sake—all moments and exchanges that I intentionally hid from my husband.

This is the antithesis of everything about our relationship. We are a team. A united front, poised together against outside threats. He has my back and I have his. Together, we are impenetrable, yet I stepped out on my own, left my back exposed and allowed this long-legged man to jump on it.

I swerve into the right lane and have to slam on the brakes, narrowly missing the back of a Tesla with a Green Day sticker on it. I jab at the horn, dive back into the left lane, and steal a quick look at the clock, ticking through Joe's schedule. He's on campus, for a lecture scheduled at eleven. After that, he'll head to the clinic.

I hesitate at the upcoming exit, then move into its lane and gun it down the ramp. I merge, then take a right at the light and pull into a parking lot. Putting the town car in park, I grab the first thing I find—a white paper bag from the breakfast shop at the corner. I dry-retch into it once, collect myself, then retch again. Everything comes up, soaking the thin paper bag and coating the half-eaten bagel and wadded napkin in a spray of cookies-and-cream ice cream that is tinged orange from my morning juice. I inhale and lift my head from the bag, catching a glimpse of myself in the rearview mirror.

My eyes are red, and there are specks of vomit on my lips. I use the sleeve of my shirt to wipe them off, but it doesn't make me look any less guilty. Is it from my marital deception or from the fear of the investigation? Maybe both.

I reach over and open the glove box, grabbing the spare napkins I keep there. I sit back and dab my eyes and the top of my shirt. There's a big glob that smears, and I want to cry from the weight of it all.

My phone lights up with a text from Joe.

I love you so much.

I stare at the screen, and my eyes blur with tears. There's my karma for always scoffing at the blabbermouths at the clinic and in my interview rooms. I haven't cried in years, not since Oley died—yet here I am, falling apart in a Toothy Smile Dentist parking lot.

I can't bring myself to text Joe back, but I need to. He'll wonder about the silence. He'll look at my location. He'll stew. Our relationship has a stack of rules, and communication is always at the top of it. Honest communication. At the reminder, a fresh flood of tears leaks out.

The phone dings again, and I know it's him, nudging me for a response, waiting outside his class, his foot tapping, irritation growing at my silence. I blink rapidly and reach for the phone. But I was wrong: it isn't him. It's Freddie.

Come back. I have to tell you something. I'll be at the north end
of the parking lot. Trust me, you want to hear this.

I stare at my phone and try to compute the message. I shouldn't
have left him there. It will be part of his report: *Detective Marino pitched
a temper tantrum and left me in the parking lot of Chunky Mike's. It was
on my walk back to the station that I got attacked by a team of meth heads
who stabbed me multiple times.*

I read the message twice, then three times. What could he possibly
have to tell me? It's likely bullshit—a ploy to get me to return so he
doesn't have to catch a ride home. Likely.

But what if it isn't?

I reach over and shut the glove box. Pulling back, I pause. On the
floorboard, pushed all the way to the front of the cavity, is Freddie's
backpack.

CHAPTER 32

JESSICA

The days all run together in here. I have no idea if this is my third day or my sixth. I'm starting to crave the medicine, wanting the fog of white and sleep that it creates.

They gave me a puzzle. It's a giant photo of a carnival, and I'm almost done with the Ferris wheel that takes up the top-right half of the board. It's two thousand pieces. I saw this video online once of competitive puzzle competitions, and I've tried to time myself to see how long it takes me to do ten pieces, but I'm literally counting seconds in my head and I suck at keeping track of it.

The nurse brought it to me, along with a sudoku workbook. She never talks to me; she typically opens a window that's in the wall and slides a tray in with food or items like this at random times. I'm normally asleep when she comes by, but sometimes I've been awake, and when I try to talk to her, she ignores me.

She's only come inside the room a few times, typically to change my IV bag or empty my trash. I asked her for tampons and to take me to the bathroom, but she ignored me. Later, she did put tampons, extra diapers, and a bottle of Midol on my tray, but all I want is a nod, a grunt—anything to acknowledge that I exist, that I am still a person underneath these scrubs.

There is something deconstructing about being ignored. It's proof that you're not worthy enough to be spoken to or acknowledged. I took a class in college on social welfare my freshman year, and one of the things we talked about was basic human rights. We separated into small groups and made a list of what we thought basic human rights included. My group had almost thirty items, and we had a pretty heated debate about some of them, like cell phones and internet access. The root of our baseline was what a homeless person deserved to be provided by their government.

Acknowledgment wasn't even a consideration for the list. Conversation and interaction with others—also a noncandidate. A toilet was, but now that I've had three bowel movements and spent hours in a urine-soaked diaper, I can confidently say that if given the choice for a toilet or a conversation with someone other than Dr. Joe, I'd go with the conversation.

It wouldn't even have to be a long discussion. Just something. Is it raining outside? How many people are at this place? Can I get group time with others? Do you guys have anything here to eat other than protein shakes and energy bars?

That's my menu, by the way. My trays contain three protein shakes and four energy bars. Oh, and a piece of fruit. I've gotten a banana, orange, and an apple so far. My fingers are crossed for another orange. The last was a big juicy navel that I took my time eating.

There's a knock on the door. It cracks a little and Dr. Joe sticks his head in. "Is it a good time?"

"Oh, no, I'm very busy right now," I drawl, putting down a four-sided piece that has a funnel cake on it. "Hot social calendar. Come back in three hours, after everyone leaves."

He steps in and smiles. "Humor. That's good." Picking up my chart, he pulls the pen out from the top of it and glances over the page, as if he needs a refresher on who I am and why I am in here. The quick perusal irritates me, because how many of his patients killed their mother? I have to be an anomaly. If I'm not—if there's dozens of us—then there's something in LA's drinking water.

"How are you feeling?" He pulls one of the plastic chairs away from the table and takes a seat next to me. His knee bumps mine, and I don't move away.

"Not great. I'm on my period. Sorry, it smells like blood in here." Super smooth on my part.

He shrugs. "I don't smell anything, but please remind me; I'll take out your trash when I leave."

"I'd really love to use the bathroom. And take another shower."

"We can move you to a different room, one with a shower and toilet, once you pass the cognitive test." He writes something down on his paper, as if he hasn't just said something big and important.

"What do you mean? What cognitive test?"

He looks back at me. "Do you remember what happened with your mother?"

"I—I . . . Why? What does that have to do with anything?"

"You're currently considered a high-risk patient. Both to yourself and to our staff. It's why you're sequestered and on a no-points restriction." At my confused look, he tucks the pen into the clipboard's holder and explains. "Nothing sharp. No pens or pencils. Forks, knives. A typical toilet has enough water that you could drown yourself in it. There's no electrical outlets, light bulbs you could break, long cords or ropes in here. This is one of our soft rooms."

All this sounds like it's for someone else. I wasn't in danger of killing myself or anyone. But they don't know that. They think I killed my mom, which I absolutely didn't. Couldn't have. I glance down at my wrists, which still hold the ugly red scars. How deep did I dig that razor? How close did I come to dying?

"Once you remember the details, can talk through those with me, with the police, then we can determine if you are in a more stable emotional state and able to be trusted with more freedoms. That's the cognitive test."

So, once I remember killing my mom, I get to have stuff.

But I didn't. I couldn't have.

"Let's start from the top. What's your name?" He tosses it out like he hasn't asked me that a dozen times, but suddenly I straighten, my body going rigid, because my brain is serving it up, right on the tip of my tongue like it's been there the entire time.

"Jessica," I say.

And just like that, as if the name unlocks something in my head, everything floods back.

CHAPTER 33

DINAH

Freddie's backpack is a slim leather one with a half-dozen compartments, the top unzipped and gaping open as I pull it onto my lap. Inside is an apple, a protein bar, a mini bottle of Advil, and a leather portfolio that is almost identical to the one I use for my daily case files.

I pull out the portfolio and open it as my phone dings with another text from Freddie. The left side of the portfolio has my internal case file, which I've never seen. I pull out the stapled pages and start to skim through them. Eleven years in the LAPD, all detailed here. My initial field scores and aptitude tests. My most recent psychological report. I flip to the shrink's notes and read them in detail.

> *Struggling with the death of her partner. In denial of the level of her grief.*

> *Doesn't want another partner, likely because of the mental trauma from Oley Hugh's passing.*

> *Mentions her husband with excessive frequency. Is likely in a codependent relationship.*

Highly intelligent and at risk of being bored in this role.
Should look for advancement opportunities to provide to her.
Will clash with personality types that are similar to her own.

All bullshit. I flip the page and see my stats. Arrests made. Warrants issued. Investigations closed. All above average. There's a reason I was promoted to detective so quickly. A reason I get my pick of precinct and assignments. I'm one of the best detectives Los Angeles County has. I'm told that over and over again, a compliment supported by my record. Yet Freddie was sent to spy on me. Why?

Next, an abbreviated list of cases; these must be the ones they found suspicious. Some of them, I understand. The investigations were messy and disjointed. Mistakes were made, clues were missed, evidence was lost. A few I am innocent of, but all in all, it's a terrifying list, one that could mean the end of my career if they dig into all of them.

My phone dings, and I pick it up and scroll through the texts, all from Freddie.

Are you coming back? I'm at the end of the parking lot.

Dinah, seriously, we have to talk. You need to know something.

I'm sorry that I didn't tell you, but I had a good reason.

He doesn't need a good reason. He was conducting an investigation. Deception is just part of that equation. I understand that. Respect it. *You need to know something.* Is it just a trap to keep me from finding his backpack and reading this folder? Probably. Joe would know. If I told him all this, the background and all the details leading up to these texts, he would be able to say with absolute certainty whether or not Freddie was bullshitting me.

But I can't ask Joe. Not without first confessing, and I'm not ready to do that.

I keep flipping pages, and the rest of it is all about Reese and Jessica Bishop. All the crime scene and lab reports are here, with Freddie's handwritten notes in the margin. Most are about me—comments on what I did properly and anytime I missed something that he caught.

I look for what I am terrified of: Car-tracking data. My cell phone records. Anything on camera records or neighborhood sweeps. I am frantic, my finger skimming over the words, and I almost miss the section at the bottom of the final page.

> IA investigation opened after a call received from Oley Hugh on September 25th. Follow-up meeting held on October 2nd. Oley is a cooperating resource in this investigation.

I stare at the paragraph, reading the lines over and over again until I have to blink rapidly just to keep my vision clear. The folder drops onto my lap, and I sit there for a moment, not moving, barely breathing, as I try to process this information.

A call to Internal Affairs, from Oley.

A follow-up meeting.

A cooperating resource in this investigation.

Shit. I begin to pant, tears welling, and I quickly press my fingers underneath my eyes, pinning them shut, and force myself to calm the fuck down and take a deep breath.

It can't be right, yet there is no reason for this folder to lie. I think of how often he came to the ranch. The moments beside me in the car, driving while I spoke to Joe on the phone. Eating lunch at Virgilo's, his hand always reaching for the check. His big goofy grin, which only dropped when we were at a crime scene or if the Padres were losing.

No one knows my secrets, save Joe—but Oley . . . if anyone was going to figure them out, it would be him.

Did he?

The question is almost worse than the idea of an IA investigation, and the thought of telling Joe about either hits me in the face with the severity of a shovel.

I carefully pick the portfolio back up and consider what to do with it. There's a round trash can at the side of the dentist's office. I could junk it, but this isn't 1990. There are digital files that back up every page in the binder. Fifteen minutes and a dozen mouse clicks, and the file will be re-created.

Okay, so I'll give it back to Freddie. Don't let him know that I've read it. Finish the Jessica Bishop investigation 100 percent by the book and pray that it satisfies their curiosities and they go away.

After that, maybe I'll retire and convince Joe to quit the clinic. We'll find new hobbies to occupy our time.

It sounds miserable, but maybe that's what life at a certain age becomes. I push the portfolio back into Freddie's bag and return it to the passenger-side floorboard.

It takes me a moment before I can stomach the energy to put the car into drive and head back to the ice-cream shop. This feeling . . . this sear of pain across my chest, the bitter taste in my mouth, the heave of my stomach . . .

I thought that my first heartbreak had broken the organ so badly that it was permanently scarred over, impossible to reinjure in such traumatic fashion. But this is almost worse. I'm not a kid; I'm a grown woman. A homicide detective. I should be able to sniff out deceit, should be able to know my friends from my foes, and the saddest part is that Oley was just about the only friend I've ever had in my life. Short of Joe, which is a different type of friendship entirely.

My one friend, and he did this to me. He suspected this of me and went behind my back to see if it was true.

Fuck him. Fuck him and fuck me for crying over his grave and for wasting years of my life thinking that I loved that man and he loved me.

I slam both fists on the steering wheel and let out a long, agonized scream of frustration. At myself. At Joe. And at Oley.

CHAPTER 34

JESSICA

"My mom's name is Reese. Reese Bishop. We live at 23 Luther Drive in Montebello. Fourth house on the left after the stop sign. We had a dog named Beau, but he died two years ago. I work at Chunky Mike's. I drive a Nissan Altima. I have like three hundred dollars in my bank account and was dating a guy named Luke, but now I'm single—or I think I'm single because he hasn't texted or called me in like three weeks, ever since we slept together." I inhale, then go to start in again, but Dr. Joe holds up his hand, stopping me.

"What's the last thing you remember? Do you remember checking yourself in here?"

I pause, my breath still captive, ready to come out, but I have no words to deliver. I puff out an exhale, frustrated. "No."

He frowns, and I hurry to speak.

"I mean, not yet. But I will. Now that I know who I am, the rest will come back. And you can call my mom, right? And see that she's just fine, it's all good, and I can go home?" I bounce in the chair, and happiness swells in my chest at the thought. Home. I know what home looks like. What our living room looks like, and my room, and the crooked picture in the hall from when Mom brought me home from the hospital— "Oh . . . ," I say suddenly. "Mom's sick. Did I already tell you that? She's, um . . . she's going through treatments." My joy leaks out of me, and I try to plug the holes before it's all gone. "But she's going to be fine. She says that she is. And she's doing pretty well. She's trying really hard."

And she wasn't dead. That must have been a hallucination of some drug I'd taken. I probably went out that night, took some laced shit, and imagined the entire thing, then became convinced it was real. I tell him this theory, and he nods slowly, his gaze holding on to me, and I hate the pity on his face. The assumption that she is dead or dying, that I'm just a dumb girl who refuses to accept that my mommy will die—but people beat prognoses all the time. If anyone can beat this, she can.

She will.

CHAPTER 35

DINAH

A marriage is a Swiss cheese block, with holes and tunnels for secrets. I end up storing the one about the IA investigation in a deep well that intersects with the last two weeks of history with Freddie. Two secrets now lodged inside my brain.

The first, which is that I've intentionally omitted the fact that I have a handsome trainee stuck like a burr to my ass during the investigation of Jessica Bishop's disappearance, is something I'll likely never share. I don't need to. It can go down as one of the minor actions a wife takes to keep the peace in her relationship.

The second is a ticking time bomb, a tunnel that cannot go unmined. I pull up next to Freddie in the ice-cream shop parking lot and practice the introduction in my head.

Something happened today. I need your help with it.

Giving Joe a problem will help deescalate his emotion. He will become fixated on the problem and temporarily lose track of how it originated.

"Look, we need to talk about this." Freddie takes the passenger seat and pulls his seat belt across his lap.

"Nah, I'm good." I pull out and into the exit lane, twisting around to see if it's free.

"I want these girls to be found, Dinah. That's all. We all want to bring them home."

I almost choke on the stupidity of that statement. Pinning my lips together, I make the left turn and head toward the station. A mile until the lot. I'll pull up in front, drop him off, then leave. If he refuses to get out, I'll . . . I'll figure something out.

He doesn't do anything that dramatic. The final mile is done in silence, the stiffness hanging in the air between us. I turn into the lot a little too quickly, and the car rocks a bit, then I'm braking in front of the building and gesturing him out.

The memory of Oley, the way he'd heaved his girth out of the car with an overly loud sigh, hit me. Had he been thinking of the IA investigation when he'd laid in his hospital bed and said his goodbyes to me? He had told me that he loved me. Hugged me. Teared up as he'd gripped my hand and stared into my eyes.

Had he considered telling me then? Warning me? Confessing his betrayal?

". . . call you."

I realize that Freddie is standing beside the car, leaning in the open passenger door, his backpack in hand.

I pull forward, and the door swings closed and clicks into place.

I head toward the clinic, driving the speed limit and using my turn signals. I come to a stop at a yellow light and realize I'm stalling.

I don't want to go to the clinic.

I don't want to return Joe's text.

I am not ready to tell him about the IA investigation.

Unlike my other secrets, this one I have to tell him. I can't bury this one for years, can't lie on top of another grenade each night, hoping that it stays buried.

A marriage may be able to handle one major deception—but not two. Not when this new one affects him also.

I park in front of the clinic. My movements are slow as I stagger out of the car and down the mulch-covered path to the back door. The facility is quiet, and I walk down the main hall and open the door to Joe's office. He's not at his desk, and I pause at the sight of him in the adjacent patient room, the view clear through the large double-sided mirror set into the connecting wall. He's seated at the room's table beside an attractive young brunette. The girl is animated, her mouth moving quickly, her hands jerking through the air. I move closer to the window, until my breath fogs the glass, studying the young woman, her thin nose, her heart-shaped face.

Jessica Bishop.

She's thinner than she looked in the photos tacked to the wall of her room. Then again, most of the patients lose weight in here. A week of drinking protein shakes and eating a low-calorie diet of fruit and snacks has likely dropped ten pounds from her frame. From here, I can see the bright-red scar on one of her wrists and remember the night she came in, the quick work that was needed to close up the cut, her blood gushing out all over the admittance-room table. She was incoherent, her words spilling over each other, tears flooding her eyes.

He's already made so much progress with her. She's smiling, her head nodding, and I wonder how much they've talked about her mother's death. Her file is compelling, the evidence hard to dispute, and maybe she's already confessed to the murder. Maybe that's why Joe is looking at her so intently, like he's fascinated by whatever she is saying.

I watch them for a half hour, then leave. Walking out the door is like coming up for air. I have a stay of execution for at least an hour—maybe two—before I have to tackle this confession.

But it isn't two hours. It's past six by the time he pulls into the driveway. I've already cooked dinner and am waiting at the front door with a smile and a kiss, just like he likes it. He starts talking as he unknots his tie and hangs his jacket on the hook, his energy and enthusiasm high. A breakthrough, he crows, and I pierce shrimp on my fork and twirl fettucine and smile and ask questions, and another hour passes before he is doing the dishes and I'm fixing us an after-dinner drink. We settle into the two chairs beside the fireplace, and there is a moment, a break in his chatter, when he takes a deep sip of his brandy and sighs.

I hesitate, not sure where to begin, even though I practiced this all afternoon.

Then he is talking again, his words tumbling over themselves in a rush to get out, and I love his passion. He's a world-class chessmaster in the area of human psychology. I sip my drink and wonder if he plans on recapping the entire four-hour session. He does that sometimes, and I never mind when he does.

Tonight, I appreciate it, even though it means that we are heading to bed at ten thirty and I still haven't said anything to him.

I can't bring it up now, not while we are side by side at our respective sinks, brushing our teeth. It'll be a discussion that will take hours and require both of us to be alert, and throwing it on him with no warning and when he's putting his mouth guard in—it's not fair. It's not fair, and I don't have the mental energy for the fight and the questions and his alarm.

So it'll have to wait until tomorrow. Tomorrow, we will drive to the ranch for the weekend, with no distractions and hours stretching out before us, open for nothing but discussion over my deception.

Tomorrow. It looms ahead of me, already waiting.

I try to sleep, but my stomach is one long tangle of knots, and no matter how much I reposition myself, I can't get comfortable.

CHAPTER 36

DINAH

Friday afternoon, we drive to the ranch, our hands intertwined on the Excursion's wide center console. I've spent all week looking forward to this one-on-one time with him to regroup and make sure that everything is as it should be. Now, with my confession hanging over my head, it feels more like a prison sentence.

Joe has Dave Matthews on the radio, and I try to relax. He's such a great driver. One hand on the steering wheel, the other in mine, his body relaxed but his attention constantly ticking through and checking the different items: the mirrors, the different lanes, the speedometer, the temperature gauges, the oncoming traffic. He doesn't speed, doesn't get perturbed by other drivers or traffic, and uses his turn signal. The ranch is only twenty minutes away, but he spends every Friday morning checking the air in the tires, topping off all fluids, and filling the tank up with gas. This morning, while he did that, I fixed us each a thermos filled with coffee and dressed for a hike, lacing up my boots with a stomach full of trepidation and guilt.

This weekend, I have to tell him. The sooner, the better.

But I don't—not right away. Instead, I melt into the passenger seat, my fingers interlaced with his, and listen to Dave croon as we leave the city and enter the suburbs, then the open desert. We purchased the ranch because of its proximity to the city. Far enough out for serious acreage, but close enough if I get called in on a case or Joe needs to run to the clinic in between classes.

I love our routines, especially our visits to the land. Joe says I need it after the chaos of my childhood, which was very much a "figure it out as we go" mindset, where plans were made and discarded on the fly and RSVPs always had a question mark at the end, in case something better came up or we forgot.

Sal loved the calamity; I hated it. I liked my pens and papers in order, my desk calendar to be accurate, and if a commitment was made, it was kept. Take a homecoming date, for instance. If someone mentioned that they would take you, then they should. They shouldn't take your sister, shouldn't force you to hide your dress and your expectations in the back of the closet and pretend they didn't exist.

"Your family still coming next month?" Joe's question is a welcome interruption, and I shift in my seat so that I can face him.

Next month. By then, the IA investigation should be done, and Jessica will likely be released. I shake off the thought and answer his question. "I don't know. You know them. Mom says definitely yes, which means it's fifty-fifty. I know you said it's okay, but—"

"It's fine. The guest cottage is ready; they'll have a nice time."

I digest the idea, one I'm not entirely comfortable with, but if Joe is, that's all that matters. He's right: the guest cottage is ready. I'll need to air it out a little. Fluff the beds. Stock the fridge. Take that ugly hat rack that Oley carved for us and move it into the main house, just to make sure it doesn't get damaged.

Oley gave us the rack a month before he passed. It's one of the best—and worst—gifts I've ever received. After his death, I moved it into the guest cottage. I had to. Every time I saw it, I was struck with my last memories of him, his big body barely fitting into the hospital bed, his smile still wide, his jokes still pouring out of him even while his heart beat its final notes.

Maybe now I can look at it without crying. Maybe I can ignore our badge numbers, which he carved into the bottom. Maybe all that will be easier since I now know that he was a traitorous asshole.

"You okay?" Joe brings my hand up to his mouth and kisses my fingers, right by my wedding band.

"Yeah." I smile, but I know he can see the sadness in my eyes. "Just thinking about Oley."

"I could grill a tenderloin next weekend, if I place the order with the butcher tomorrow. We could do the same when your family visits."

The abrupt change in topic is a familiar tactic he uses with his patients—the reprogramming of your mind away from a painful or harmful thought. I appreciate it, and I let my mind tick over to all the things we need to do to prepare for our upcoming guests.

Mom has been trying to visit the ranch ever since we bought it. We typically beg off visitors, blaming the hunters that lease the ten thousand acres of forest around it. But with the guest cabin done, I finally caved after six years of resistance.

"I wish she wasn't bringing Marci." I turn my air vents off.

"You act surprised that she is. You know Marci's her favorite."

It's the truth, but I wish he wouldn't say that. It would be nice for my husband to at least pretend that my sister and I are on even footing in this one remaining aspect of our competition. I should be winning in any competition with my mother as judge. After all, we don't borrow money from her. We take her on trips, invite her to dinner at our homes, and create moments like this upcoming visit—one where she won't have to lift a finger and will enjoy all the comforts of home, thanks to the extensive and expensive renovation we just completed, all with her in mind.

"The bigger question is, is Marci bringing Eric?" Joe squeezes my hand and then disentangles himself, and it takes me a moment to realize that he wants me to let go. I do, and my hand immediately feels small and insignificant as a result.

"Marci isn't bringing Eric. He has to work." Thank God. The only thing worse than dealing with my mother and Marci for a weekend is to have them both preening over Eric and listening to him try to keep up a conversation with Joe.

"Okay, so they'll be fine, just the two of them in the cabin. Not too crowded." He doesn't comment on Eric's absence, but I know he's happy he won't be there.

"A tenderloin would be nice." I reach down into the floorboard and fish out a clip from my purse. I stick it in my mouth and twist my hair into a messy bun, then use the clip to secure it in place. "We could play Scrabble one night. Mom would like that."

"Sure. I'll keep an eye on the weather, but it should be nice." He glances at me. "You're nervous about something. Is it the ranch?"

I shift in my seat. "I mean, partly. Marci is always looking for something to be wrong, something she can jump on and pick apart. I don't even like the idea of her coming on the property, much less exploring—" I break off at the thought of my nosy sister peeking in our bedroom, of the look on her face when she sees our separate beds, the "his and her" division of the room. "I don't want them in our house, like at all."

"Well, that's why we built the guest cabin," he says. "So we could have our own space. They're two grown women; they understand our need for privacy." He gives me a crooked smile, as if we will be rocking the bedposts and don't want my family listening in.

But the truth is, it doesn't matter if Mom and Marci are in the guest cabin or the bedroom adjacent to ours. Joe and I aren't that kind of couple. What we have goes so much deeper than the crude connection of sex. Granted, maybe it could be even deeper if we ever introduced that aspect into our marriage.

Maybe. I've always wondered if it would. If we could try—just once—and see.

CHAPTER 37

DINAH

A few miles from the ranch, I check my messages. Nothing from the station or from Freddie, who has gone silent since I dropped him off.

Thank God. He's the last person I want to hear from. Such an incredible waste of time, having to hold his hand through the investigation. And for what? Him to spend that time leaving breadcrumbs just to see if I'd follow them?

It was disrespectful of my time, and of the women we were investigating.

I used to call Oley at this point in the drive and let him know that I was checking out for the next two days. I would spend the time to catch him up on any open cases and reinforce the transfer of responsibility. Oley was my comfort blanket, in a unique way that Joe couldn't be. While Joe protected me personally, Oley was my shield and cushion professionally.

Was.

Now I feel like I'm going through the job without armor. I've been telling myself for years that I was paranoid about the exposure, about the feeling that I was constantly at risk—but now look at where I am. Deep in shit.

Joe slows, putting on his turn signal, and I tuck my phone into my bag and roll down the window, hanging my head out as he turns onto our private dirt road.

I love the ranch—absolutely everything about it. The way this entry is rutted and often washed out, a journey that leaves its mark on our cars, the dried brown splashes on the wheel wells and fenders an oddity in a city like LA. I love the smell of the air—free of smog and entitlement, thick with pollen and evergreens and damp leaves and dirt. I love how we have a rusty gate at the entrance with an old-school chain and padlock, just past the mailbox that says MARINO in white paint with a heart next to it. I painted that mailbox. I sat at the dining table while Joe lay on the couch and watched football, and a chicken casserole was in the oven and the smell of it was heavy in the room.

As I painted it, I thought about all the possibilities on the acreage. One day, a collection of animals in the north barn. Air-conditioning in the south barn. A dedicated work and research space for Joe. A painting studio for me. At the time—six years ago—I saw myself an undiscovered talent, one who might explode on the art scene under a pseudonym and ridiculous price points.

I'd planned out a series of paintings, each one titled after a missing person. It would bring awareness to the crimes and be a great PR pitch for the art.

Unfortunately, my painting skills never developed much further than block letters on a mailbox. Joe hammered the post into the ground and attached the mailbox. Every few months we empty it and dump all the political mailers and junk mail into the trash. It's useless, but I love it and everything else out here, and how different it all is from our home. It's like we live in two different worlds, carry on two different lives, similar only in that we fit perfectly together inside both.

Joe comes to a stop just before the padlocked gate. Reaching up, he pushes the button on the remote that's clipped to the top of his visor, and the entire gate, padlock and all, clicks into motion. Another secret of the land, just like the electric fences that run along the entire perimeter.

As the gate fully retracts, the dirt path stretches ahead, framed by giant oak trees with heavy woods on either side. It looks quiet and peaceful, and I lean over and impulsively kiss Joe on the cheek. "I'm always so happy to be here," I say, and maybe I will wait until Monday to tell him about the investigation.

"Me too." He takes his foot off the brake, and the vehicle rolls forward.

CHAPTER 38

DINAH

I wake up on my side, and it takes a moment for me to place where I'm at. The ranch bedroom comes into focus in the dark. I roll over onto my back and wait, listening.

There is no sound from Joe's side of the room, and I prop myself up on my elbows, looking over at his bed. My eyes adjust, and I can see that his white sheets are pulled back, his bed empty.

The bathroom off our room is dark, the door cracked. I consider using it but lie back down and close my eyes, willing myself to return to sleep.

It's not going to happen. My legs are starting to twitch, and I'll need a glass of milk to fall back asleep. I sit upright, swinging my bare legs over the side and tapping my feet along the floor, looking for my slippers. They are lined up by the bedside table, and I slip into them while holding on to the edge for balance.

I'm in cotton underwear and a big shirt of Joe's, one that advertises a seaside town in Washington we visited a few years ago. It's chilly in the room, thanks to the window air-conditioner Joe installed out of fear of our central system going out. It was intended for emergencies, but it gives the room an extra kick that he likes. I grab my big, fluffy white robe off the hook on the back of the door and shrug into it, then quietly make my way out of the room and down the hall to the kitchen.

The ranch house was built in the '50s and is a typical low-ceiling box, one devoid of any character or frills. The original owners were farmers, hence the slaughterhouse, chicken coops, barns, and paddocks. This farm didn't include the surrounding acreage, which was all timber and hunting land that Joe bought up, parcel by parcel, until we owned almost two square miles.

My family isn't aware of Joe's money. If my mother knew how much is in our investment accounts, she'd faint. Joe's father was the majority shareholder of the country's biggest hot sauce company, a fact I didn't know myself until he gave me an unlimited budget for our wedding.

My mother and family think our bills are paid from my job and Joe's positions at the college and the clinic. My mom would faint a second time if she realized how little he brings home—which is one of the reasons why I would never tell her. I like his titles and the important work he's doing. Hundreds of students thrive under his tutelage each semester, and in the future, he'll be known worldwide for his research and papers on the effects and effectiveness of thought reform and coercive persuasion.

It doesn't matter if he works pro bono. That doesn't indicate his worth or his contribution to so many lives. I know that better than anyone. Had I been assigned a different mental health counselor during my struggle with the Blythe Howard situation, I probably would have quit the LAPD by now. Definitely wouldn't have stayed on homicide.

I shuffle into the kitchen, which is a galley setup with two counters separated by an eight-foot gap. The floor in this part of the house is all original wood planks that are as uneven as a four-year-old's teeth. I open the fridge and take out the half gallon of milk, checking the date on it before pouring a tall glass. We'll need to do a grocery run before next weekend, so I open the junk drawer and remove the notepad and pen to make a list of what to buy. Joe has already written down a few items: bleach, garbage bags, bagels, lighter fluid, and sea salt. He also wrote down charcoal, but I saw a bunch of bags in the back of the Excursion, so I cross that off.

I add milk, as well as a few of Mom's favorite items while they are top of mind. I'll ask Marci to send me a list, too, so I'll know what to get but also what to avoid. I can't keep track of her allergies, which seem to multiply each year.

The window above the sink is dark, and I glance at the stove to see what time it is. 2:48 a.m. Another four hours until sunrise. This sink is the best spot in the house to see it rise. I spend most weekend mornings standing here, a warm mug of coffee in hand, watching as it peeks over the tree line and paints the back fields and barns in a warm glow. We don't use the barns close to the house; they are all empty—future projects if we ever move here full-time and can support animals. I want a pig and some goats and maybe one of those little furry mini Highland cows. For now, we only use the old slaughterhouse and the larger barns on the edge of the farm. I'll head out there after breakfast to check on things, but for now I turn away from the window and pause, listening to the sounds of the house.

There is no movement, only the soft click of the grandfather clock in the hall. The living room, with its big heavy couch and recliner, is quiet, any potential sounds muffled by the rug and the wall of bookshelves and paperbacks.

I know, even without checking the other two bedrooms or the laundry room, that Joe isn't there. I carry my glass to the door off the kitchen and slide it open, stepping out on the wooden deck, but he is not out here either. The outdoor dining table is empty, as is the seating cluster by the small firepit. I sniff the air to see if he is burning anything out by the barns, but the air is clean and quiet.

The parking spots by the house are empty, which means he's likely taken the Excursion down to the clinic, if not off on an errand.

I turn and close the door behind me, leaving it unlocked. I tilt back the glass, finishing off the milk, then rinse the glass out and put it in the dishwasher. Padding back down the hall, I enter the bedroom, slip out of the slippers and robe, and return to bed.

It's not my business where Joe is. He knows where our bedroom is. If he needs me, he can call—but he won't.

CHAPTER 39

DINAH

In the morning, Joe scrambles eggs and fries bacon. We have the window open over the sink, and there's the twitter of birds and the rustling of pine needles every few moments with each strong breeze. I'm sitting at the round kitchen table, a copy of the *Los Angeles Times* spread out on the table, a pencil in hand, the Saturday-morning crossword puzzle stretching across the page.

"Three letters. Symbolic embrace."

There is a pause with just the scrape of his spatula against the pan and the crackle of bacon.

"Hug."

I write it down, but it seems too basic. I go to the next one. "Sixth-amendment guarantee. Nine letters. Second letter, T."

"Attorney." He turns down the burner and opens a cabinet above the stove, grabbing two plates. "These are almost done."

I put down the pencil and pick up my cup of coffee. "You need a top-off?" I slide the paper to the side, clearing a spot for us to eat.

"Nah, I'm okay." He scoops half of the eggs onto a plate and turns from the stove, placing it at his spot on the table. I like my eggs without a hint of moisture in them, so he leaves mine in the skillet while he transfers some of the bacon to a paper towel–topped plate. He cooked two pounds of bacon, way more than we'll ever eat, but we'll take the extra to the clinic and share it with the patients. It's a Saturday-morning tradition, one that will allow him to fit in some sessions, and me to help out for a few hours.

I press on the top of the Keurig and consider mentioning his absence last night. Not because I don't trust him, but because I'm curious how long he was gone and if he was having trouble sleeping. He used to have problems with insomnia and restlessness. I haven't heard him complain about it recently, but I also haven't woken up to an empty room in a while.

"Did you want to run up to Bottle Cap tonight and have a few drinks?" He turns off the burner and transfers my eggs to the plate.

"That sounds good to me. But it's Saturday, so you know Lucy will try to make you sing." The coffee maker starts to gurgle, and I watch as a stream of steaming black espresso falls into the white mug.

"Oh, that's right. Karaoke night." He winces, like he doesn't like it when the bar's owner begs him to get up onstage.

He loves it.

He loves it for the first half hour while he protests and refuses, insisting he's just there for a few drinks, not to make a fool of himself.

He loves it while he downs beers and flips through the book of song selections, all while continually insisting that he won't sing, that the ones who do embarrass themselves.

He especially loves it when Lucy takes the mic in between performers and points him out in the crowd and tells the bar that Dr. Marino will put everyone to shame if they can just convince him to get onstage. And then I'll start to clap and chant, "Dr. Marino," while he scowls at me and shakes his head and calls out, "Absolutely not," before Lucy jumps off the stage, runs over, grabs him by the arm, and pulls him up to the stage.

Only she isn't really pulling, and she and I and every employee of that bar know the game. They all know that Joe loves the show and that his bar-tab tip will be four figures long, and that his voice is above average at best and certainly not worth all the whooping and hollering they will do.

And he'll preen and blush and come back to the table with a big smile, one that will last all night, and it will be worth every dollar of the tip and every minute of the act.

I play the game because I love him. It's the same reason I work at the clinic and helped him build it from the ground up. There are certain things that rev my husband up. The cheers of the crowd at Bottle Cap. The respect of the patients at the clinic. The rapt faces of his students at the university. The unwavering support of his wife.

"If we head up there early, we can leave before karaoke starts." He grabs the pepper shaker and seasons the top of his eggs.

"Sounds good to me." I steal a piece of bacon off the top and crunch into it as I take my seat. "Bacon's delicious, babe."

He nods as if it's nothing, but the corner of his mouth twitches into a small smile. If he were a piano, I'd have him tuned to perfection.

CHAPTER 40

JESSICA

It feels like ages since anyone has been in here. I'm worried because I had a window of clarity and now I feel like it's gone. When Dr. Joe left, he gave me my meds, and everything sort of washed away. The only way I can tell how much time has passed is how loopy I still am and how many diapers are in my bin.

I think the protein shakes they give me also have something in them. When I leave here, I'm going to file a complaint against the facility. I mean, diapers—really? The nurse mentioned putting in a catheter when I complained about them, so I shut up real fast. But I feel like the diapers are a psychological tactic, something else to degrade us, to break down part of our soul.

I still have my strength, despite the horrible food and the diapers and the lack of mental stimuli. The sudoku book they gave me is ridiculously hard. I'm only about 70 percent through the first puzzle, and I'm pretty sure most of it is wrong. I'm over half-done with the carnival puzzle and I'm getting faster at it, so maybe they'll have a different one I can do after this one.

I've never wanted a therapy session so bad in my life. When Dr. Joe left last time, he promised to look up my mom and have them do a wellness check on her. So when he comes back, I'll be able to confirm that she's okay—and she'll know where I am so she won't have to worry about me.

Maybe we'll go into his office again. We did that on the third or fourth time I spoke to him. The room has all these rich textures; everywhere you look there's something else to see. The soft leather of his couch. The wood panels on the walls. There's this supersoft blanket on the back of a soft plaid chair. Then there are some small knickknacks you can see if you look closely. Like this bronze horse statue on his desk and some glass awards on the bookshelf. I picked up this candle that was by my chair and smelled it, and it was like a fir-vanilla scent that was so good I just kept sniffing it during our session like I was a drug addict or something.

The only thing weird about his office is the window that looks into mine. I kept looking at it and trying to think about what I had done in my room that he might have seen.

If we go in there again, I won't look at the window. I won't even touch his candle. I'll just bask in the soft glow of the lamps and maybe borrow that soft blanket to wrap around my shoulders, and answer all his questions and hope that he just lets me stay there for the night. I could definitely sleep on his couch. Use the bathroom that's right outside his office door. Read some of those books that are lining the walls.

Instead, I am stuck in this stupid white box. I cram a puzzle piece with a red balloon into place with more aggression than is needed.

There's a rap on the door, and I turn from my spot at the table and sag with relief at the sight of Dr. Joe, who steps in wearing jeans, a T-shirt underneath his lab coat. He's also wearing sneakers. It must be the weekend.

I have to say, I prefer the suits. He rocks them with deadly precision, a look that has grown on me the more I see him. He's pretty hot. He's got a light sprinkle of gray hair above his ears, and his eyes are super intense. When he stares at me, I can tell he really is listening to me, and I'm not sure that any man has ever really stopped talking long enough to hear what I have to say. And his lips kinda tilt to one side when I say something he likes. I live for those smiles. Each session, I try my best for one. I'll take the small ones, but the really special moments are when he releases a full-blown grin. Once, he laughed, and I think the action caught us both off guard.

He's the type of man I'd like to marry. My mom will love him. She is always going on and on about high-value men and that I deserve the best that is out there, and blah, blah, blah. She would fall over from joy if I came home and told her that I was dating a doctor. Not that I would date Dr. Joe. I mean, to be honest, I would—if he was single. But he's not, and he has never given me the slightest hint that he's interested.

"Good morning." He closes the door behind him, and it clicks into place. He's holding a plate wrapped in foil, and I inhale the familiar smell of bacon. Today there's some stubble on his face, and I like it. It makes him look a little more rugged, like a sexy doctor lumberjack.

"Morning," I chime, then pause. "It's morning?"

He checks the Rolex on his wrist. "10:42, so yes. How are you feeling?"

"Groggy. Bored. Is that bacon for me? Did you find my mom?"

"Yes, the bacon is for you, and yes, I found your mom." He glances at the half-completed puzzle, which is taking up most of the table. "Please, sit back down, and let's chat."

"We could go in your office if you want more space?" I suggest. Please, please, please.

"No, it's probably best if we stay here." He places his clipboard on the table and opens his hand above it, dropping three white pills on its surface. Then he pulls a bottle out from under his arm and sets it beside them.

It's fruit punch Gatorade. A simple, dumb thing, but my eyes fill with tears at the sight of it. My mom always says my blood is half Gatorade, I drink so much of it. And fruit punch is my favorite. Gatorade and bacon. I'm so happy I could die.

"You told me this was the flavor to get." He takes the chair next to mine. "I'll bring more tomorrow."

I don't remember telling him that, but half of our sessions are a blur to me. "Thank you." I pick up the bottle and twist off the cap, then put the pills in my mouth and wash them down with the drink. I chug half of it, then come up for air and peel the foil off the paper plate. There's a small pile of crispy and curly bacon—the good kind, with lots of fat. "What did my mom say?"

He moves aside the clipboard, and there's a thick file underneath it that I haven't seen before. "I received this from the police department, Jessica."

Jessica. My name sounds like a death sentence on his lips, and I don't like this vibe at all. He's got this flat look on his face, and then he nudges the file toward me with the tip of his finger. *I received this from the police department.*

The police department.

I set down the piece of bacon I was about to put in my mouth. "I can open it?"

"Yes, please do."

I sit back in the plastic chair and pick up the file.

CHAPTER 41

DINAH

I'm sitting in the clinic's lounge when my cell phone shrills loudly, Freddie's name on the display. I silence it and wonder how deep my culpability is.

The good news is, the LAPD is investigating this. If the department is horrible at anything, it's assembling a case for prosecution. I might be fired as a result of this investigation, but they would have to dig really deep to find any obstruction of justice or witness tampering . . . and honestly, what detective doesn't do both of those things on a regular basis? Every detective I know does. Oley did. Hell, Oley taught me how to cover my tracks.

And then he called and turned me in. He wouldn't have done that over something small. He knew what an IA investigation does to a detective's reputation and career. If he took that step, it means he suspected me of something heinous. Something worth going against the credo of the blue shield.

I rise from the couch and stretch, then slide my cell phone into the pocket of my hoodie. Turning off the television, I drop the remote on the couch and push on the swinging door to the kitchen area and storage room.

I need to just confess all this to Joe and see what he says. He'll know what to do. He'll form a strategy and hire an attorney and have them tap-dancing so much they won't have the time or the awareness to catch me in anything.

That's the smart thing to do: push back and stand my ground. An innocent woman would be offended and aghast at the idea that my performance is being questioned; she wouldn't dodge calls and hide in the break room of her husband's work. I move through the kitchen and stick my head into the hall, double-checking that Joe is still in with Jessica.

The patient across the hall is singing, her voice warbling through an Adele song that used to be popular. I tune her out and listen for a hint of what is happening in Room 1, where we put the new arrivals.

It's quiet down there, and I glance at the clock that hangs at the end of the hall, calculating how long Joe's been in there. Almost twenty-two minutes, in a session that will last at least an hour. I pull the door closed.

I should call Natalie first. Our chief is a bitch on steroids, and she loves a fight. Whether or not she'll be on my side is up for debate, but she'll want to know this as soon as possible, so I might already be too late.

I pause at the fridge and open it, scanning the contents for something to calm my stomach. Each patient has a section, their medicated smoothies lined up in neat rows, all prepped and ready for the weekend. The bottom shelf holds the good stuff, and is reserved for staff and the occasional treat for patients. There's an eight-pack of red Gatorades there, and I twist one free, then grab a raspberry yogurt out of the drawer. I get a spoon, then take one of the seats at the table and peel off the lid.

I pull my phone out and scroll down to Natalie's name in my Contacts. I initiate the call.

She answers on the second ring, her voice shrill and cracking, as if she's been up all night screaming at someone. "Marino, what is it? I've got a dead hooker in Santa Monica whose coochie I'm staring at right now, and Belkis doesn't know his ass from his armpit."

I inhale, then let it out. "I just found out that IA is looking into my cases."

She lets out a string of expletives, then pauses for a moment. "You certain?" she finally asks.

"Yes." I dig the spoon into the yogurt. "I've had a trainee following me around on a suicide I'm investigating for Rita Perez. Turns out he's an agent for Internal Affairs."

"What's his name?"

"Freddie Hodgkins."

"And he was shadowing you on the . . . Is it Reese Bishop?"

"Yeah."

"Well, that's pretty cut and dried," she says flatly. "Nothing to get you on there, especially if we find the daughter."

I put the spoon in my mouth. Finding the daughter is not going to happen, at least not on a timeline that will help with my investigation. I swallow a mouthful of yogurt, and a knot of stress in my chest relaxes a little at the confirmation that Natalie's on my side. Calling her seems to have been the right move.

"I just want to keep you in the loop," I say, "and see if there's anything I should do."

"Yeah, don't help them out," she snaps. "I'll call the union and get you a rep. Stay superclean on the Bishop case, you hear me? How deep are they digging in your past cases?"

"Ummm . . ." I try to remember which names were on the folder in Freddie's file. "Some of the ones are a few years old. It's a bunch of my unsolves."

"Fuck them and their grandmas. Show me a detective in this town without unsolves. Better than false convictions. I swear, they aren't happy unless we're eating shit and smiling. Okay, let me get on it. But don't forget what I said, 'kay? Super squeaky on Bishop. Everything aboveboard. So far aboveboard your tits are in heaven. And focus on the missing daughter. Find her and make a splash when you do. Press conference, lots of photos—you know the drill. Call Kelsey in publicity and have her go big."

I look at the patient board, where each name is listed in neat alphabetic order along with their admittance date.

Jessica Bishop is the second name.

Everything aboveboard. My tits in heaven. Find her and make a splash.

"Okay," I manage. "Got it."

"All right, stop yakking so I can call the union and deal with this hooker. Let me know as soon as anything happens."

"Will do." I hang up the phone and stare at Jessica's name, then sigh and heave to my feet. Chucking my yogurt into the trash, I push through the door and out into the hall.

CHAPTER 42

JOE

I take a break from the patient and walk down the hall, glancing in the windows of the other rooms. Everyone is quiet and calm, save for the screams that are coming from Room 4. Thanks to a careful regimen of medication, the rest of the rooms are behaving or sleeping. No time to check in on them now, not when we are mid-breakthrough. The cocktail of drugs I gave Jessica will be working right now . . . loosening the grips that a mind puts in place, the ones that block receptive thinking and lock memories in staunch order. I'll give the medicine an hour to work, then show her the photos of her mother again. And this time, the results will be different—I'm certain of it. If not, I'll wait a day and then pursue the more aggressive methods.

Either way, Jessica Bishop will eventually accept a memory of her mother's murder. It might take a few days or, as in the case with our more stubborn patients, a few weeks. Occasionally, it takes months—but that was in the early days, before I'd honed the process.

Now it's much easier, and my success ratio is almost 100 percent.

Jessica will break. It might even happen today, and I catch myself smiling at the possibility.

The screams are louder as I near the door at the end of the hall. I withdraw my keys and flip through them for the one to her door.

Melonie has been one of the more resistant and problematic patients from the start. It wasn't entirely a bad thing; it allowed me to better shape the psychological profile of individuals who will or won't respond to forced reeducation techniques.

I fit the key in her door and unlock it, then step inside. Her screams falter as I pull the door shut. Turning, I regard the forty-two-year-old woman chained to the outside wall. In the last two years, all her muscle tone has melted off her large frame, leaving a shell of the landscape architect's original physique. Her hair is streaked with gray and matted from her repeated attempts to thrash against the wall. Her bucket for feces and urine has been knocked over, and the smell of her waste is thick in the air.

I meet her eyes and we're both tired of this fight. "You'll be released tomorrow," I say.

She doesn't believe it. Her body tenses, and her face wars between relief and distrust.

"I'll be back in a few hours to check on you and undo your restraints so you can sleep in bed. In the meantime, try to rest. Screaming isn't helping anything." I open the door and return to the hall, locking her room. It's unnecessary, given her restraints, but still—procedures are in place for a reason. While it's often easy to forget those reasons, it doesn't make them any less important.

I swing by the break room, looking for my wife. She's not there, so I check my office next and find Dinah curled in one of the chairs, a paperback in hand. She and I are both reading the Magdalene series, which is based in Scotland in 1920 and about the various crimes of a Protestant Glasgow razor gang. She's ahead of me; she tucks a bookmark in her spot and closes the book, unfolding from the chair at the sight of me.

We always vowed, from the beginning, to prioritize each other over everything. If I am watching or listening to something, I pause it when she comes in. If I'm on a phone call, I end it to accept her call. If I'm with a patient, I step out if she needs me. There is nothing in the world more important than the other person. Everything else can wait. Anything or anyone else can be inconvenienced for our relationship. Priorities are the difference between failure and success.

"How's it going?" She walks over and wraps her arms around my neck, pulling me against her chest.

"Good. I think it's going to be a breakthrough day for the newest patient."

"That's fantastic." She curls her hand against my chest, fisting my soft cotton shirt. "What would you like for lunch? I was thinking of making some chicken salad. I could make you a croissant sandwich or put it in a salad?"

"A sandwich would be nice." I press my lips against hers. "Thank you."

"Of course. I'll run to the house and do that. There're snacks in the kitchen if you need something before then."

There's something off about her, and I grip her tighter when she attempts to leave. "What's wrong?"

"Nothing." She pats my chest but doesn't try to pull away again. "I'm just starving."

I stare into her eyes, reading them. They are clear, her expression calm, but I can sense the stress radiating from her. Maybe it's from Jessica being here. It isn't standard for us to have a patient with a connection to one of her cases, so I can understand the strain it must put on her. "You sure?"

I hold my breath, hoping she will share her feelings, admit her weakness, but I know my wife. She is a tight vault, one with a complicated combination to unlock. I don't have the time for that right now, but later, I will. It's important that we share everything, big and small. I tilt forward and kiss her again, inhaling at the touch of our lips together.

When we break apart, it feels like a loss.

"See you in a couple of hours." She steps back and grabs her novel from the chair, dropping it into her canvas tote. She plucks one of Jessica's Gatorades from the small gold table beside the chair. I purchased an eight-pack of the sports drink, and I wonder how many my wife has consumed. We are not near a store; there is not a convenient way to replace them this weekend. I press my lips together at her carelessness.

She moves past me and into the hall, and I take a moment and use the sleeve of my lab coat to wipe at the ring left behind by her drink.

CHAPTER 43

JESSICA

My mom is dead. I stare at the photos and don't understand why I am so calm. My mind is ticking, like a clock progressing forward, the facts each presented and absorbed. *Next.* I mention it, and he says the medication I'm on will numb those feelings, to not worry about it.

I can't worry about it. The medication has numbed that part of me.

So, Mom really is dead. Dead. I've never known anyone who has died before. I feel the sadness, but it feels like it is calling to me from far down the beach. It's faint, almost carried off by the wind.

She was my best friend. I'm not sure how many people can say that, that their mom was their best friend. When I turned eighteen, moving out wasn't even a thought. When I started college, I stayed in my room, and probably will until I get married. We have an easy relationship, Mom and me. She is just the right amount of discipline and soft. I've never done anything bad because I respect her too much.

I remember when we got the news of her advanced heart disease. I sobbed for days. I was in a fog, but not like this one. It was more a constant cloud hanging over every interaction, every task, every conversation—one that consistently reminded me of what might happen. I didn't care about anything but that. I didn't want to do anything but spend time with her. Try to help her. I've spent the last three months *terrified* I will lose her.

And now it's happened, and I am just sitting here, turning pages in a folder and trying to remember if I already ate lunch. I think I did. I remember a Gatorade. Was there something else? Real food? I think I'm hungry, but maybe I just want the activity of food.

"It's important for you to understand what you did, Jessica."

He's handsome. I think I've mentioned that before, but each day he gets better. I think I hit on him. That's also faint, but I definitely said something about his looks. Reached for him. Offered something. All I can remember is the sting of rejection. It made me like him even more. We spend so much time alone. He could have tried anything. Said anything. I bet patients in here offer him blow jobs for real food, maybe even more than that. But he's such a gentleman. He has a wedding ring on his finger. Lucky woman. I wonder if she really appreciates him. I didn't appreciate Luke enough. Wait, not Luke. Luke is that prick who slept with me and then went MIA. Who is the other guy? The one from Chipotle? Henry. Oh my God, Henry. He was *so* sweet. Too sweet, Mom said. She said that's why I was bored with him, and she was right. But maybe I was wrong. Maybe I should call him when I get out of here. Let him take me to that pottery class he kept inviting me to. Maybe that's what I need. That would make Mom happy—not that she will know.

I can't believe he is letting me look at this folder. Is this good for my psyche? It's all photos of my mom, her face slack, vomit coming out the side of her mouth. Off medication, I would be sobbing and throwing these pictures, then rushing to grab them because they are horrible but they are her, and should be protected at all costs. Especially in here, where I have nothing to remind me of her, nothing to remind me of anything. If I focus on the edges of the photo, if I place my thumb over her face, it's just a photo of our kitchen. I like our kitchen. We painted the cabinets together, just like a year ago. She let me pick the color, and I went with a pale purple that she said was mauve, but I argued it was lavender.

In these pictures, she's seated at the round table just off the fridge, her body bent forward, head turned to one side, cheek resting against the crossword puzzle. She loves crossword puzzles; it's the only reason we subscribe to the *Los Angeles Times*. Each morning, she completes the daily, often calling out clues as I rush around the kitchen, grabbing a bagel and heading out to class or work.

"I don't understand," I say. "This says she died of poison."

"I need you to try to remember," he says again, like he hasn't said this a dozen times already, like I'm not straining every blood vessel in my head to try to remember.

"You've blocked the memory because it is a painful one." He turns the page and shows me the toxicology report, one we've already gone over three times. "Pentobarbital is what was given to her. You likely put it in her orange juice. You told us that you ordered it online." He flips the page and shows me a receipt from MedsUS.com with my name and address. There was only one item ordered: fifty milligrams of pentobarbital.

"I didn't do that," I say emphatically. But did I? My mind swims over the possibility. It seemed insane when he first broached it. Now, after days and days of thinking over it . . . maybe I did. She was in pain. She was hurting. She was, despite everything that she insisted to the contrary, dying. Maybe I did it to stop her suffering. Maybe.

"I'd like to read you the statement from the officer who admitted you on Tuesday." He sits back in his seat and turns over a new page, pulling a set of reading glasses off the top of his head and positioning them on his nose. "Female is highly emotional. Continually states that she needs to be fixed and that she wants to kill herself. Has deep lacerations on her wrists indicative of a suicide attempt. When asks if something happened, she states that she killed her mother. Becomes highly agitated and combative when asked for details. Says that it doesn't matter, that she's dead. Female refuses to give her name or any personal details. We administered a sedative and confined her, took fingerprints and DNA and submitted them to law enforcement."

I listen numbly as he talks, and it sounds like another person he's referring to. I look down at my left wrist and carefully trace my thumb over the wound. There are neat sutures along the cut, black stitches standing out from my pale skin. It feels hot and itchy, and when I press my finger against the incision, the pain is a little dizzying. "Am I going to be arrested?"

A dumb question, but I don't understand why no one has shown up yet and taken me away. I confessed to this crime. I wet my lips and realize they are salty. I touch my cheek and realize it is wet. I am crying, and maybe I have been for a while. Emotion. It ticks past me and is already out of reach. I am torn between telling him to take me off these meds and appreciating the cushion they're padding me in.

"Right now, my focus is on helping you get better. Think of your brain as a Chinese checkerboard. You had a traumatic event"—he taps the folder—"which was tantamount to slamming a fist down on that board and causing all of your marbles to pop out of place. Some just bounced into different spots on the board, but others rolled off. They might be nearby or might have rolled under a couch and require a little more hunting. My job is to help you find the different marbles and make sure they get put back into place. Think of facts and acceptance as different marbles. Today's marble is the fact that your mother has died and how she died. That's the marble we are working on today. There will be plenty of time later to talk to the officers."

He smiles, but there's nothing here to smile about. This sounds like a lot of work, and any thoughts of going to a pottery class with Henry next week are starting to sound unrealistic.

"How long will I be here?" I shift in my seat, and the diaper squishes against my skin. Not soiled yet, but I consider my bladder and the idea of peeing right here, right now. I've never peed in front of him before, and the idea is appealing. He won't even know it is happening.

"I'm not sure. We have some patients that have been here years. Others only take a few weeks. It just depends on each situation."

Apparently, I killed my mom and tried to kill myself. Sounds like a bad situation.

Years.

I can't stay here that long. No. Absolutely not.

CHAPTER 44

DINAH

I bring him lunch and we eat in his office, then head back to the house. Joe is wired and talking nonstop, his energy high. I play into his good mood, smiling at the right moments and chiming in with comments and questions, but my heart isn't there. I keep wondering if I should interrupt and tell him about my conversation with Natalie.

Natalie called me today. Internal Affairs is sniffing around my older cases.

That's all I would need to start with. He will have lots of questions after that, and I wonder how many of those I will have to answer with lies.

"She's a nice girl, you know. Has an inner sweetness. Reminds me a little of you, actually." The Excursion bounces over the dried-out juts in the road. We really should have a grader come in and make this smooth.

Reminds me a little of you. I press my lips together, hating that statement. When we met, when we married, no one reminded him of me. I was unique, special. Has that faded? Is it a physical similarity or a personality one?

I won't ask him. I don't want him to think any deeper about her—not right now. Not when I have so many lies around this IA debacle that I am going to have to put into careful order and deliver with precision.

I *hate* lying to him. Each lie is a string, one that wraps around my neck, joining the big rope that's already there. The noose is over two decades old, one I carried into this marriage and that has been steadily tightening in recent months. Add enough of these new strings to it, and it'll strangle me to death.

He can't find out about that rope. I'm close to cutting it free, but a few more things have to fall my way first. This IA investigation and Jessica Bishop are the opposite of what I need right now.

"I showed her the photos, and the acceptance is already there, Dinah. I'll start to taper off her meds tonight and let her have an emotional release, and tomorrow we'll do another long session. I have to say, the new combination of drugs is so much better. I can already tell the difference. I might start to try it on the older patients with smaller test topics."

He should give up on the older patients. There's only so much you can do to someone's soul and psyche before they check out. It's already happened with a few of them, but I get that he doesn't want to waste any opportunities.

"I would wait on tapering off her meds. Give her another day." I put my hand on the seat belt's buckle, unclipping it as the SUV rolls to a stop in front of the garage.

As always, my husband considers the input. "What are you thinking?"

"It's a big hit you gave her today. I would let her rest up. Allow the emotions to come to her gradually. You won't be able to make progress if she's a grief-stricken wreck."

"Part of that emotional break opens the door to acceptance," he points out.

"Speaking from the standpoint of a woman who has a complicated relationship with her own mother, trust me on this." I place my hand over his, squeezing.

"Okay." He yields, in part because I rarely have an opinion in any matters concerning his patients.

I let go of his hand and open the car door, stepping out. I think of Jessica, her profile as she sat beside him at the table, so close they were almost touching, their knees together under the table.

She's a nice girl, you know. Has an inner sweetness. Reminds me a little of you, actually.

A memory of myself flashes, standing outside his office, obsessively running my hands through my hair, my palms sweaty, my heart pounding in my chest. I was such a child with him in the beginning. So impressed by the diploma on his wall, the concepts he spoke of, the way he understood—really understood—my anger over the Howard child and my fear that the mother would get away with murder.

"Hey." He stands at the front of the vehicle, keys in hand, his expression intent as he studies me. "You okay?"

How many sessions has he had with Jessica? Five? Ten? Too many.

The noose is getting too tight around my neck. It's time for it to be put around someone else's.

CHAPTER 45

DINAH

Joe twists open a beer and takes a sip from the bottle, then places it on the arm of the Adirondack chair. It's dark, the only light coming from the illuminated steps going down to the yard and the citronella candle that's on the small table between us. We didn't make it to karaoke. That possibility was thwarted by Jessica Bishop's domination of my husband's day, a development that he talked about throughout dinner prep and execution. The only benefit is that Joe was so enamored with it that he didn't notice my distraction, and there was never a pause to bring up the Internal Affairs debacle.

There's a long pause now, one filled with the soft jingle of the porch's wind chimes. I take a sip of my own drink, a chilled glass of rosé. It's from a vineyard in Agoura Hills; Joe makes the hour-long trek every other month or so to get me a fresh supply.

I don't like the wine. I did, during the three-hour tasting tour we took there. I got absolutely trashed and remember hanging on Joe's arm and giggling as I gushed on and on about their rosé. Sober, it tastes like pond water with a hint of alcohol. I hate it.

But I love that he goes there just for me. I love that it's a recurring item on his calendar and that he doesn't forget, that he pushes clients to the side and fits it in around his class schedule and makes it a priority in his life because he thinks that I like it. That, I can drink to. That makes it worth the weak taste and lingering dry mouth. My plants seem to like it. At home, I dump my wineglasses into their pots when he isn't looking, and they've thrived as a result. My ficus has a dozen new buds and is positively bristling with the drunken confidence of a bar hag.

"Tomorrow I'm going to repot the tomato plants. They're outgrowing their containers." I stretch my legs, and the blue-plaid pajama pants I'm wearing ride up to expose my ankles. A mosquito seizes the opportunity, and I reach down to smack it. Blood smears, and I wipe it off with the pant leg. The PJs were a gift from Marci, her Christmas shopping reduced to scrolling down a page on L.L.Bean's website and one-clicking a set for each family member. Joe refuses to wear a uniform of any sort to bed, and is currently in dark jeans and a long-sleeved shirt. Tonight, he'll sleep in just his boxer briefs, his covers thrown off, his body hot no matter what the temperature in the room.

"That salsa you made was really good."

The salsa was a new recipe from Mom, and just the thought of her upcoming visit causes my stomach to cramp. When Mom picked the date for their trip, I didn't expect to have a mountain of stress pressing on my chest. Another reason to have the Jessica Bishop situation cleared up. The original plan—to give Jessica time to confess to the murder, then release her from the clinic—is going to take too long, and every additional day that she's here, the risks increase.

I didn't think there was any danger in Joe working with her, but look at what he said earlier. She reminds him of me. Look at how much time they are spending together. A four-hour session today. Four hours he could have spent with me.

My husband is not a stupid man. My history with Reese Bishop . . . he could figure this out if given enough pieces of the puzzle. It is my job, as it's always been, to make sure that doesn't happen.

"Can you make more?" Joe looks over at me. "Another batch of the salsa?"

I nod in agreement, thinking through the proper extraction of Jessica. "Tomorrow night, how about I make lasagna? I'll do an extra pan for the clinic also."

"Sounds delicious. Need me to pick up anything from the store?"

"No, I have everything I need here. I'll defrost the hamburger meat tonight."

He closes his eyes and reclines back against the chair, a small smile on his face. I'll crush a pill and put it in his portion of the lasagna. He doesn't like ricotta, so I always prepare a smaller pan for him. The flavors will cover up the taste of the pill.

I forward to the next song on the playlist and look up at the sky. The night is clear, and a thousand stars are overhead, dotting the dark.

Quiet perfection. Too quiet to mar with the IA discussion. Plus, I have a more important task ahead of me: keeping our perfection intact.

Inside, tucked in the pocket of my windbreaker, my phone vibrates with a text message.

CHAPTER 46

DINAH

I wash the dishes from our breakfast and consider the knives as I clean them. There are scalpels at the clinic; those are what I should probably use, but it seems strange to have a small paring knife, the edge razor sharp, and not stick it in the pocket of my shorts. This one here, the one with small watermelons printed on its blade, has a matching purple sheath. I fit the point into the sheath and slide it into place, then tuck it into my pocket.

The smell of his huevos rancheros still lingers in the air. I made fresh salsa to go with them, my mother on speakerphone as I sliced the tomatoes, her calling out the recipe items to me as I went. There's a little left, so I spoon it into a plastic container and put it in the fridge beside a bag of grapes.

He comes up behind me and slides his arms around my waist, pressing his mouth against the back of my neck, and I think of all the looks we get from other couples. The envy on the wives' faces. They all want what we have. The spark. The respect. The bond. But they don't understand what is required to keep all that intact.

Most of them would never put in the work required. They couldn't. They aren't built for it.

Tomorrow, I'll put in overtime, with a task that will be my hardest, but it will be worth it, for this. I lean back into his hold and turn my head, kissing him on the lips. He smiles against my mouth, then pulls away, and for all my husband's perceptivity, he doesn't suspect a thing.

Hell, for the last month, the master of analysis hasn't realized that his wife has woken up each day with an anchor on her chest, barely able to breathe. Ever since I got the first email from Reese Bishop, I've been drowning.

Joe was in the kitchen with me, slowing stirring a pot of bisque, when my phone first chimed with the notification. Everything in my body froze at the introductory line of Reese's email, and I excused myself to the small powder room we had built underneath the high part of the stairs. I read the email three times, then ran the sink to hide the sounds of me vomiting.

I have always sworn that Joe and I are impenetrable, but I know, each time I've said it, that there is one thing that could knock us apart.

One thing Reese Bishop knew.

Between the risk that Reese told Jessica and the girl's increasing proximity to Joe, I have to remove her from the situation, no matter how difficult that act will be. I plunge my hands back into the hot water and grab the sponge.

Tomorrow night, all this will be done, and the only thing to do will be to handle the aftermath of my actions.

CHAPTER 47

JOE

On Sunday, I spend almost four hours with Melonie, and when I come back to the house, there's a little blood underneath my nails. I scrub them in the kitchen sink and listen to see where my wife is. There's music playing faintly and the smell of fresh flowers, so I follow the scent and the sounds and find her in the greenhouse off the back deck. It's about the size of a two-car garage, and packed with flowers and vegetables of every variety. There're two paths that intersect the space, and she's in the middle of one of them, on her knees, her hands deep in the soil around a zucchini plant.

She's singing along to a Billy Joel song, which is playing on the radio of the old boom box that sits on the table along the outer wall, right next to a large glass of iced tea and a collection of hand shovels and shears.

My wife has a horrible voice. It pitches when it should soar. It finds keys that haven't been discovered yet. This song is kind to her—"We Didn't Start the Fire"—as it is really more of a chant than a song. She knows every word, and it's a joy to watch her rapid-fire delivery, her chin rocking to the beat as she recites it without taking a breath. She hears me and turns, a grin stretching across her face as she rises without pausing, her volume increasing in tempo with the song as the second chorus approaches. She stalks toward me, her energy growing until she is bouncing in place before me, her arms extended, palms out, and it's a beautiful thing to watch, my wife so full of life and joy as she belts out the chorus with unrestrained enthusiasm. I join in on the familiar refrain, both of us united in our insistence that we didn't start the fire.

I don't dance—it's not in my DNA—but I spin her in a circle and do a half shuffle, smiling as the smock she's wearing flares out along with her hair, a top of curls and canvas. Underneath the smock, she is in cut-off shorts and a thin white tank top. She's tan from our weekend hikes, her body toned and strong, her freckles visible on her makeup-free face, and this is the Dinah I love the most. Weekend Dinah, away from her caseload and her uniform—her spirit wild, heart happy, her focus entirely on us and this time. I pull her to me and kiss her, and she grins against my mouth, nipping my bottom lip before pulling away. "Fill that bucket?" she calls out, pointing to a yellow bucket at the end of the aisle. Bobbing her head to the next song's beat, she returns to her spot and drops to her knees.

I pick up the bucket and carry it into the kitchen, where I put it on the floor next to the sink. Pulling the long hand sprayer from its spot by the faucet, I stretch it out and hang it in the bucket, locking it into place and letting it fill while I use the bleach spray to wipe down the counters.

Melonie didn't bleed a lot. I double-check my shirt and pants carefully, but the disposable jumpsuit I wore on top did a proper job of protecting them. Killing is a task I never enjoy but one that is necessary—the retirement of a piece of equipment that has outlived its usefulness. Besides, now we have an open room, one that Jessica can transition to as soon as she accepts and admits that she is responsible for her mother's death.

She's close. I'm willing to bet it will happen tomorrow.

I take the paper towels I used and push them deep into the trash, then pull the bag out and double knot it at the top, setting it by the back door. All our ranch trash goes into the fire bin. I'll start the burn in the afternoon, and add charcoal to the bin to disguise the smell of burning flesh. There's usually a chill in the air when the sun sets, so it will provide some pleasant warmth while we hang out on the deck and listen to music and grill steaks.

I haven't had to burn a body in a while, but this week is an exception, which is why the bin is almost overflowing despite its large size. It'll take over two hours for the fire to break down the body to bones. I'll put cedar and more charcoal on top of the bones so that it'll smell good by the time Dinah joins me. Before her family comes next week, I'll go on a hike and bury the bones a mile or so out into the woods. I can fit an entire body in my camp pack. The skull starts out as the biggest bone but is easy to shatter into smaller parts once it burns long enough.

I turn off the water and return the sprayer, then carry the bucket back to my wife. She is now in the throes of a Toto song, wailing to "Africa." I set it down and our eyes meet, and she smiles and I've never been so in love with her.

CHAPTER 48

DINAH

The lasagna is ready and cooling on the stove, 20 mg of clonazepam ground up and sprinkled between the layers of his portion. I stand at the window, coffee cup in hand, and watch the smoke rise from the back of the slaughterhouse. He's been out there for hours, feeding trash into the large buckets. As soon as the flames die down into containment, he'll leave it and walk up to the house, working off his big canvas gloves one finger at a time as he approaches.

The motion light on the right side of the house comes on, and he appears, his long shadow stretching forward and bobbing along the grass as he heads this way. I move away from the glass door and enter our bedroom, passing through and flipping on the light to the bathroom, my movements quick and practiced as I turn on the shower and drop a bath towel into the warmer.

I'm settling into my recliner in the living room when Joe stomps on the mat and pulls open the slider. Leaning forward, he loosens the laces on one boot and then the other before stepping out of both of them and into the house.

"Shower's running," I call out. "Hurry, dinner's getting cold."

"Bless and thank you," he says. "I'm a mess."

He looks it. He's covered in a layer of ash and soot and stinks of smoke. Ducking through the room, he beelines for the shower.

I fix our plates and am pouring him a glass of red wine when he comes out of our room, his hair wet and messy, his skin pink, smelling of the pine-and-eucalyptus body wash he orders online. It costs a ridiculous amount but is cocaine to my nose.

"There's still a couple of hours left in the burn if you want to sit out there after dinner." He pulls out his seat and grabs a paper towel off the roll in the center of the table.

"Actually, I'm exhausted." I place his plate in front of him and take my own to my spot, snagging my fork off the table as I settle into the seat across from him. The lasagna is still hot, and I use the edge of the fork to section off a piece, the cheese stretching as I pull it away from the rest. "I think I'll take a hot bath and then hit the bed."

He nods, his jaw already working, his fork quick as he stabs at the stack. He's always starving after working outside. There's something about the fresh air, the manual labor . . . I could have burnt the lasagna to a crisp and he would still inhale it.

I slow my eating, taking time to sip my wine in between bites. As I watch, his plate empties until his fork scrapes across the china. I rise. "Want more?"

"Yes, please." He picks up his wineglass, and between the merlot and the pills, he'll be asleep in an hour, maybe sooner.

I reach for his plate and hope he doesn't notice the way my hand trembles.

CHAPTER 49

DINAH

The clinic's security lights turn on automatically when the nose of the Excursion edges into the spot by the front doors. In my pocket, Joe's phone buzzes with the notification of the security system. I withdraw the device, dismissing the alarm. I'll need to clear the event from the log, but I can do that once everything is done.

I use my key to unlock the front door. It swings open silently, and all the lights are out, the hall a long swallow of blackness. I flip on the lights and walk past the patient rooms, quietly counting as I move. Only five patients right now with yesterday's checkout. Five patients, one remaining problem.

I stop at the supply room and squat to see the third shelf. Needles and syringes. Alcohol swabs. Suture kits. Scalpels. I select one of the larger ones, then straighten and also get a vial of pentobarbital.

I stuff the items into the pockets of my hoodie and leave the light on. Propping open the door so I have some illumination, I walk down the hall and stop outside the last door on the left, adjacent to Joe's office.

All the rooms are secured the same way, with a double-sided lock. I work my key into the slot and pause, collecting my thoughts.

Can I do this?

It's the first moment of hesitation I've allowed myself to have. I knew what would happen when we brought her here. I orchestrated it. Chose her. This was her fate from the beginning; I'm just shortening her sentence. It's mercy, if anything.

She won't feel anything.

Won't know anything.

More importantly, she won't be able to tell anyone anything.

Joe will be furious. All this effort, wasted. His forward progress, gone. All his bubbly energy will turn into rage. It will be messy and loud and long.

And then it will be over.

He will return to his other patients. I will return to work and the investigation. I think of Natalie's last voicemail, with instructions to meet the union rep tomorrow at 11:30 a.m. and a stern directive to not be late. As if I would. Joe and I will leave here in the morning, despite Jessica's dead body, and return home so I can work and he can teach his class. He'll come back later in the evening and deal with the aftermath, and by Tuesday, it'll be as if it never happened.

The tight rope around my neck: gone.

Already I can breathe easier. I turn the key to Jessica's room and push open the door.

CHAPTER 50

DINAH

She is sleeping on her side, and stirs when I enter but doesn't wake. I leave the door cracked so some of the hall's light comes in.

Her dark hair is a mess on the pillow, and for the first time since she was admitted, I take a moment to really look at her. She's got long lashes. A thin nose with a slight bump. Some acne scars on her cheeks. I think of my own acne, which flared to maximum levels that summer I was away. She's been drooling, and I stare at the dried saliva and resist the urge to wipe it off.

She is a problem, I remind myself. That's it. A problem that needs to be eliminated. I can't think of her as a person.

Instead, I think of Joe. The tender brush of his fingers across my cheek. Our future. Him going gray. The afternoons we will share. The trips we will take. We have decades ahead of us, decades that could be destroyed by this one thing. This one problem.

Reese Bishop is taken care of. Now for the last piece of the equation.

Her hand with the IV port is tucked under the pillow, and I reach for her arm and pull it. She startles at the touch and opens her eyes, her body tensing.

"It's okay," I say softly. "I just need to give you some medicine."

She lets me take her hand and I turn it over, checking the IV. It's still in place, though it will need to be changed in the next day or two.

"No pills?" She sounds groggy, and I'm not sure if it's from sleep or the effect of whatever Joe gave her earlier. That should be wearing off, and I check my watch as I twist the IV tube into place. 12:17 a.m. I have plenty of time.

I reach into my pocket and close my hand around the small glass vial of pentobarbital. It will take a few minutes; then she'll be out and I'll be free to do what needs to be done.

I withdraw the vial and connect it to the IV, watching as the clear solution pulls through the line and toward her hand. Now to sit and wait.

"Are you the nurse?" She clears her throat and shifts on the bed into a more upright position. I watch her but don't move to help.

"Yes."

"What's with the outfit?" She gestures with her IV-laden hand to my hoodie and sweats.

"I just came in for this. We forgot to give it to you earlier."

"So, no Dr. Joe," she drawls, and I can hear the disappointment in her voice. I don't blame her. Anyone would be attracted to Joe. He's the most beautiful man in the world.

"No consult tonight, no. You can relax and go back to sleep." I pat her arm despite myself.

"Wait a moment, please. Do you have a sec?" Her voice is so small, the question a plea.

"I've really got to go," I say, but I don't move from my spot by the bed. Her eyes are fully open now, studying me, and I feel naked without the face mask that I typically wear in the patient rooms.

"Wait, I *know* you." She straightens, and how she knows anything with all the drugs in her system is beyond me.

"Yes, I've been in here before. I brought you tampons." I should leave, let her drift off to sleep alone, but my feet seem to be rooted to the tile floor.

"No, I mean outside of here."

I'm shaking my head, but she grabs my arm, squeezing it. "You know my mom. Reese Bishop."

My mom. Reese Bishop. I thought of the scrawny woman sitting across from me at the Italian café, her long fingers pushing the contract forward.

I've kept my portion of it. She and her defective heart haven't.

"I've seen the file on her death, but I don't know her." I reach down and peel back her fingers. Any moment, the vial should start to work, and her eyes will get heavy, her grip weak. Right now, it's a vise, and maybe that's what five hours a day of scooping ice cream gets you. Cavewoman hands.

"She showed me a picture of you once and told me about you."

My throat closes at the thought. "Couldn't have been me."

"No, it was. I'm scarily good at remembering things."

Go figure. What's with Chunky Mike's employees and photographic memories? I yank my arm free and check my watch. 12:21 a.m. Talk about time passing slowly. "I'm going to step out. Go back to sleep." I stand and head out.

"I didn't kill her, you know."

I pause halfway to the door. "I believe you."

"Can I tell you a secret?"

Oh, the six words no detective—or woman, for that matter—can resist. I turn, certain that no matter what the secret is, I already know it. "Yes?"

"Dr. Joe says that I did it, but I told him I didn't, and between you and me . . ." She lowers her voice and now, finally, her eyelids are starting to droop. "I . . ."

I don't know what she was about to say, and it doesn't matter. Her mouth is open, her breathing loud and smooth, and I wish Joe slept like this. As it is, he's a silent snoozer. No snoring, no deep breathing, no hint if he is alive or dead, awake or asleep. Early in our marriage, I would sneak over to his bed and rest my head on his chest in the middle of the night, just to make sure his heart was still beating.

I withdraw the scalpel and place it on the tray beside her bed, then reach for the plastic clipboard Joe left for her. The photos from the scene are clipped in next to the autopsy reports and faux witness statements. I flip through the pages, stopping to study the fake receipt from MedsUS. com that I created on my laptop. It looks good, and I can only imagine how confused she was when she saw it.

I unclip the items and, with a swift downward motion, I smash the broad side of the clipboard against the edge of the footboard.

She doesn't stir at the loud sound, and I crouch, picking up the bright-orange shards of the plastic board. There's a nice jagged one with a sharp point, and I choose it and bring it over to her bed.

Her wounds are healing, the skin knitting together beneath the sutures. I keep the scalpel handy but use the broken piece of plastic to slice along the seam of the stitches on her left wrist. Joe and I did this to her a week ago, our shoulders brushing against each other as we worked side by side in a continual thread of connection. I held her down while he cut from the underside of her wrists to her forearms, deep enough to draw blood but not too deep to sever important tendons. Then the repairs, our breaths commingling in the air above her, me stitching the seams closed while he dabbed the blood that seeped out.

This time, there will be no repair.

I reopen the cut and then reach for the scalpel to dig deeper and sever the veins and arteries that will drain her body of blood. Before I start, I take just one short moment to look at her.

I don't have words for the mix of emotions that I feel, and maybe this is that protective instinct that so many crow over. I don't know her; she is a stranger, a distance I've made sure to preserve despite her time in this place. But still, there is some invisible hand on my chest, telling me to stop.

To wait.

To protect.

To save.

I *could* save her. I could let her out of here and take her home. I could make sure that she grows old and has her own family and realizes her dreams and fights for them. I could do that, or I could kill her now. Extinguish that flame and everything her heart and soul beat for.

Killing her is the smarter path, a painful action now that will erase a lifetime of future problems. I clear my throat and steel myself, then tighten my grip on the scalpel and carefully bring it to her wrist.

I push the razor-sharp metal tip into the cut. Okay. One quick downward yank, and it will be done. I don't have to be careful. I don't have to worry about vital tendons or going too deep. The deeper, the better. The opening will fill with blood, and in just a few minutes, she'll be gone.

"Dinah."

I jump at his voice and whirl around to face the door.

Joe's in jeans and a T-shirt, spare keys in hand, staring at me as if I have done something terrible.

"What are you doing here?" I breathe, trying to think of an explanation for why I'm here.

He shoulders past, knocking me out of the way, and I stumble, catching the wall to keep from falling. He checks Jessica's IV, her pupils, then her wrist, and I try to pocket the scalpel, but he turns before I can and catches the motion.

"What the *fuck* are you doing?" he seethes.

I have no good explanation and am out of time. "She—She . . ." I gasp for air and pull myself to my feet. "She's in love with you," I manage. "You should hear her talk about you. She's planning to seduce you, Joe. She told me all about it."

He looks down at her wrist, and even with just the opening of the stitches, it's beginning to bleed. "Since when have you had to worry about that?"

This must be what drowning feels like. Flailing in place and not finding the surface. Choking despite every effort to open your mouth.

He has to believe me. I was worried she would take him from me. That's why I'm here. He knows how much I love him. It is plausible, if not out of character.

He turns to face me, and at this proximity, he towers above me, his face dark with anger. "Answer me," he orders. "When, in all our time together, have you ever worried about me stepping out?"

Stepping out. Such an old phrase. I watch as he reaches into his pocket, and I try to sort out the right words to sell him on the scenario. "You're right," I manage. "It was stupid of me. You're just so perfect." I grab his arm, my eyes filling with genuine tears. "I'm so sorry. I was just so afraid of losing you."

A truth, mixed in with all the lies, and my anger swells suddenly at *her*, lying there in the bed, the source of all of this. "I'm so sorry," I repeat.

"Oh, Dinah," he says, his voice sad. "I'm going to need more than that."

I don't understand, right away, what happens next. Why my butt cheek clenches with a sharp pain, why Joe is suddenly so close, pinning me to him, his features intense, his gaze tight on mine.

Then I realize what he's done and I let out a sob—not so much from the pain, because that is slipping away, everything softening. No, the sob is for what is to come.

My husband doesn't drug a woman unless he plans on treating her, and I cannot—will not—become his patient.

CHAPTER 51

DINAH

I know as soon as I open my eyes where I am. The scent of Melonie is still on the sheets, her stench wrapped around me, strands of her hair still on the pillow. I try to shove off the mattress but can't. My wrists are strapped to the bed's rails, my ankles in the same constraints. I lift my head; at least that's free. I whip my head to one side, then the other, trying to see if he is here. It's hard to see anything in the dark, and it takes a moment for the room to come into focus. The shackles hanging off their mounts in the wall. The table in one corner. The chair by the door, empty. Where is he?

Maybe he's in with her. Panic wells, and I thrash against the bed and scream his name as loudly as I can. He cannot talk to her. Not about me.

You know my mom. Reese Bishop.

What had her mom said about me? Why hadn't I asked her?

Because she was about to die. Dead women tell no tales. If Joe had just been five minutes later. If I had been five minutes earlier. How long was he standing behind me, listening? When did he leave the house? Was he even asleep when I snuck out?

Too many questions, and they spin through my mind, making me dizzy. Or maybe not—maybe it's the drug. I've seen a lot of patients coming off pento, and I've always dismissed their complaints, their pleas for water and an Advil. Now I understand the problem. My headache is blinding, and I sob, then scream his name again, wincing at the bolt of pain that rockets between my temples as a result. My mouth is leathery and dry, and my stomach twists in a threat to vomit.

Joe won't keep me in here. He can't. I am not one of his patients. Natalie is expecting me to meet with the union rep today. *Don't be late, Dinah.* If I don't show up, he'll call her. She'll . . . what? Will she suspect something is wrong?

Probably, but her suspicion certainly won't be that I'm locked in my husband's mental institution.

It doesn't matter, because he's not going to keep me here. Any second, he will open the door and let me out. He probably just wanted a moment to make sure that Jessica is okay and I have a chance to calm down. We will talk, and this time, I will say the right thing. I can do that. No one knows him better in the world. I have spent almost a decade playing him like a piano. This is just a new song, one I need to learn. It can be done.

I look down and flap my fingers in the air, trying to see my hand, but the angle is too steep. It doesn't matter. I can feel the IV tape pulling at my skin, the dull pain of the needle. The fact that he IV'ed me is not a good sign. That portal can be used for anything. Nourishment. Liquids. Drugs. Poison.

I stare at the door and will it to open.

Any minute. We will talk, and then we will leave here and go back to the house, and everything will move closer back to our norm. He just needs a moment to check on her and for me to calm down. That's all this is.

I try not to think about the fact that I am tied up, a development that is not necessary and doesn't fit well into my expectation that he and I are about to leave here hand in hand.

It doesn't matter. He will untie me and remove the IV.

He will.

CHAPTER 52

JOE

It doesn't take long for Jessica to wake up, and she jerks upright with a loud gasp.

"Easy, easy." I carefully push her back. "It's okay. It's just me."

"I had a dream. The nurse was here." She coughs, and I pick up the bottle of water and pass it to her.

"Drink this."

She obeys. It's been a joy to treat this one. Never rude. Never complains. I've had some problem patients in this place. One smeared her feces all over the wall. Another stripped down naked and begged me to do disgusting things to her body. So many hostile moments. So much unappreciation. So much work, and all for no recognition, save my updates to Dinah.

I think of my wife, now sequestered in Room 4. Twice, I've heard her scream for me. It's a new sound from her, and one that I don't like. I have spent our entire relationship cherishing her. This is a situation that should have never happened, and all due to her actions. Sneaking out of our bedroom. Taking my phone. Endangering the life of my patient—and why?

It's a question that needs to be answered, both by her and by Jessica.

I smooth the hair off the young woman's forehead and look into her face. Once again, I'm struck by the similarities in the two women. The same strong jaw. Wide mouth and lips. The same thick, dark hair. Jessica looks into my eyes, and it's like looking into a mirror of Dinah's.

"Thanks for the water." She passes it back to me, and I set it on the table.

"It wasn't a dream; the nurse was in your room. I need to know what you talked about." I pull the chair up to the side of her bed so that we're at eye level with each other.

"Nothing really. She gave me my medicine. I asked her to sit with me and talk, but she didn't want to."

"She says that you are in love with me. Is that true?"

She snorts. "No." She covers her mouth with an awkward laugh. "I mean, not that you aren't cute. But, uh, I don't know. You're kind of old for me. No offense."

"None taken." I force a smile and think of all my students—college girls her same age—who trail along after me, blushing and flirting. I am an attractive man. Always have been. I spend a lot of time and money in an effort to dress and look well. I do it because it is my commitment to Dinah and because of her commitment to me. We both understand that our spouse is an extension and reflection of ourselves.

I pick up her hand and place my fingers on her pulse point, noting the smooth beat. "Are you lying to me, Jessica?"

Her face twists in incredulity, and she starts to giggle, then stops. "What do you mean? About liking you?"

"Yes, for one. Did you say anything to her about being attracted to me?"

She rolls her eyes. "No way. We've never even talked prior to this. And like I said, she just gave me the medicine and then tried to leave. The only other thing we talked about was my mom."

"What about your mom?" I keep my voice light and calm, the way I do in sessions.

"Oh, she knows my mom. I mean, she pretends she doesn't, but that's a lie."

I study her features. I've made a career out of reading people, the talent one that requires careful manipulation of my own facial reactions. Jessica is telling the truth, her pulse slow and steady, her features honest and relaxed. She has no idea how important her responses are, or how close my wife was to killing her. If I had been five minutes later, she would be dead.

She knows my mom. She pretends she doesn't, but that's a lie.

I know everything there is to know about my wife, but I don't know this. I can tell you the dates of her last menstrual cycle. Her mother's middle name. The names of her office fish. The brand of anchovies she prefers. Her favorite author. Her blood type. When her car's next oil change is due and her hairdresser's name. An hour ago, I would have bet my life that Dinah had no knowledge of Reese Bishop prior to Jessica's admittance to the clinic.

I didn't question Dinah's selection of Reese and Jessica, but maybe I should have. Maybe I should have questioned the history of every one of my patients in the last six years. "How did Dinah know your mom?"

I'm unprepared for what comes next, the brunette delivering the line with the offhanded accuracy of a seasoned sniper.

"Well, they're sisters."

CHAPTER 53

JOE

It's impossible that Dinah and Reese Bishop are sisters. I almost say it, but the first rule of psychology is to let the patient speak, so I pin my lips together and wait for her to expound. She doesn't, her gaze drifting off to the corners of the room.

I wait, silently counting to ten before I speak. "I don't understand. Your mother and Dinah were siblings?"

"Yep. Estranged. Mom says they got in a fight when she was in high school, and Dinah moved away for college and they never talked again."

Thump. Thump. Tha-thump. Her pulse, steady and strong.

Her gaze returns to me. "I know it's probably like the middle of the night, but could I have something to eat?"

"Of course." I stand and walk to the door, appreciating the moment to think. She's having delusions, which might be a side effect of the sedation. Not common, but not necessarily uncommon. I walk past Dinah's door, and it's quiet in there. What is my wife doing? Thinking, no doubt. Her beautiful little mind will be ticking through all the possible angles she will take when I step back into the room. I'll have to think several moves ahead to spot her deception as soon as she delivers it.

There will be deception. She is drenched in it. If she wasn't earlier today, then definitely now. I think of this morning, of her standing at the sink, her hands in the soapy suds. She glanced over at me and didn't smile. Not right away; the smile snuck up on her, like a mask she forgot to affix. I chalked it up to an off moment, but my wife has been a very busy little bee, and I'm beginning to wonder how much of her honeycomb is constructed of lies.

An hour ago, when I woke up in our bedroom, my first thought was that Dinah was in the bathroom. I had waited, my irritation growing at the amount of time she was spending in there. Then I stood and walked over to the door, listening for her before knocking and pushing it open. Empty. My confusion had turned to alarm after a tour of the house and the outside deck. Alarm turned to anger at the discovery of my missing cell phone and vehicle.

I took one of the mountain bikes here, my anger ramping up with each pump of the pedals. It was both a relief and a concern when I got to the clinic and saw the Excursion parked in front. There was no good reason for her to sneak out and come here, but it wasn't until I entered and found the meds cabinet open, a vial of pento missing, that I grew suspicious. I took a second vial and filled a syringe out of an abundance of caution, one that proved valid.

But still, I hadn't expected to use it on my wife.

I hadn't expected to find her with a weapon in hand, leaning over one of my patients.

Is this what happened with Tricia Higgins? Healthy one day, dead the next, her overdose on benzodiazepine troubling, given our strict control of medication.

Is it possible I don't know my sweet wife as well as I think?

I open the fridge and take a beer from the bottom shelf. Cracking it open, I tilt it up to my mouth. As the ice-cold liquid rushes down, I remind myself of how ridiculous Jessica's statement is. Dinah cannot be Reese's sister. It's a genetic impossibility. Reese is almost fifteen years older than her. Dinah's mother would have had to get pregnant at thirteen in order for the math to work, and if there is anything I know about Dinah's battle-ax of a mother, it is this: First, that she waited until her marriage at age eighteen to lose her virginity. Second, that she would never give up a child. Not that woman, whose entire life revolved around her children.

Still, there is the uncanny resemblance between Dinah and Jessica, the latter a miniature version of my wife. A familial connection would explain why I feel such a sense of familiarity with the young woman. Mannerisms and voice inflections have been proven to be hereditary, showing up even in cases of adoption, where the parent never has any contact with the child.

I finish a sip, and the rush of alcohol numbs my brain for a moment, pausing the thought process. I need to dress Jessica's wounds. Restitch her up. I think of what would have happened had I been a little later. She would have been bleeding out, and I would have used the blood packets that we keep in the secondary fridge. Jessica is O positive, which makes things easy. Same as Dinah.

What was Reese?

I take another long sip, then close the fridge and go to the file cabinet in the corner of the room. I open the top drawer, pull out Reese Bishop's file, and lay it out on the table, flipping through the pages until I find what I want. Blood type: B positive.

I set down my beer, then drop into one of the chairs.

B positive.

A B-positive parent cannot birth an O-positive or O-negative child.

Reese Bishop is not Jessica's mother.

She knows my mom. She pretends she doesn't, but that's a lie.

Mannerisms and voice inflections have been proven to be hereditary, showing up even in cases of adoption, where the parent never has any contact with the child.

Jessica is O positive, which makes things easy. Same as Dinah.

It's all there, but it can't be.

My wife, sneaking out to kill a patient. Another impossibility I would have sworn against with my life.

I pick up my beer and consider its remaining weight, then finish the contents in one long swallow. I know Dinah intimately.

Now I know her motives.

And the truth is unforgivable.

CHAPTER 54

DINAH

Joe doesn't come back into my room. I wait, my body tensed and ready, a dozen explanations quick on my tongue, but the minutes tick by, and then it has been at least an hour with no sound at the door and no light in the room.

I don't understand. We are a unit, a team. When I need him, he's there. When we fight, we work through the problem until we find a solution.

We do not go to bed angry. We do not use childish techniques like the silent treatment.

My husband loves, above everything else, to work through and discuss feelings—to death, if necessary. It's one of the most frustrating things about him, my exhaustion heavy by the time an argument is finally resolved, but right now, I'll take it. I'll take anything just to explain my carefully curated version of the "truth."

He'll be thinking over how Jessica got here, why I brought Reese Bishop to him, looking for places where this situation turned wrong. I need to be smart, to use this time to prepare to defend every lie I've told.

Thankfully, he didn't ask a lot of questions when I brought the mother-daughter duo to his attention. He needed a new patient, and I had the solution—a terminally ill woman with a daughter who could disappear without drawing too much attention. Joe loves a challenge, and getting a loving daughter to admit to her mother's murder was one he immediately embraced.

I promised him that it would be easy, and it was. Reese had no security system at her home, a flimsy lock on her back window, no dog to alert when I lifted the sill and crawled in. I let Joe in through the back door, and we went to Jessica's room first. He soaked a rag in chloroform and pressed it over her mouth, easily holding her down when she jerked awake and began to struggle.

The struggle didn't last long. Just a few seconds, and then Jessica was limp and he was carrying her out of the house and into the back of the minivan we had rented for the occasion. The white minivan, which was almost a carbon copy of Reese's and parked beside hers in the driveway.

While Joe checked Jessica's room for any sign of our visit, I entered Reese's bathroom, where her medication had been lined up, ready for her to take in the morning. I used a small needle to inject the barbiturate into two of the gel caps in the pile. Then, to be safe, I opened the lid of the vanilla-hazelnut creamer in the fridge and emptied the rest of the syringe there.

She only needed to take one of the pills or fix a cup of coffee, and it would be done. Slow breathing and sleepiness, a loss of coordination, followed by death. She never woke up, never heard us, never even knew we were there.

I could have stayed until the morning, could have made sure that it happened, but truth be told, I didn't need Reese to die. We had Jessica, and what I really needed was to keep the two women from each other.

I count to a thousand and scream his name. Count again, and repeat. I count to ten thousand and back down, then spend a long time trying to do the math to figure out how much time has passed. At least fifteen thousand seconds. That's about four hours, best I can calculate, and it's unlikely he's talked to her for that long—which means he's left me here.

I don't know how to process that, and when I finally fall asleep, it's on a pillow that reeks of a dead woman.

CHAPTER 55

DINAH

When I wake up, the overhead light is on, and I blink rapidly, trying to see better. A crusty film sticks some of my lashes together, and I carefully rub my eye with my forefinger, trying to separate the lids.

Oh, my hand is free. I sit upright and realize that my restraints are gone, along with the IV line, though the port and needle are still embedded in the back of my hand. I swing my legs off the bed and wince at the firework of pain that radiates through my temples.

A bottle of water is beside the bed, and I drink it quickly, some of it leaking out the sides as I guzzle it down.

Okay, I can do this. I take an assessment of my surroundings. No restraints. He must have drugged me at some point in the night or early morning, which means my time frame is fucked. Is it lunchtime? Afternoon? Morning? I'm in the same clothes as before, the sheets still filthy, evidence of Melonie throughout the room. Her trash on the table. Her garbage can half-full. A few empty bottles of protein smoothies stacked by the sink.

At least she was in one of the more equipped rooms. There's a toilet, thank God, and a sink. No mirror—not that I want to see what I look like right now.

I test my footing, aware that often dizziness and retching is a side effect of pento, if that's what he gave me. My legs are solid, so I straighten up, then look to the door. The butler's window beside it has been opened, and there are two protein drinks in the basket there.

I approach the basket and crouch down, picking up a bottle and turning it over.

Dinah Marino is written in neat black Sharpie on the label. Joe's handwriting.

Underneath it, the words I really don't want to see:

Patient 14.

CHAPTER 56

JOE

My wife starts to scream, and I rise from my desk and go around to my office door, shutting it to block out the sound. Glancing at the clock, I retake my seat and pick up the pen, anxious to finish this report before I need to leave for my Monday-morning class.

I am unsurprised at my wife's reaction to her containment. Dinah is a strong woman, most similar to Patient 8 from a few years back. Patient 8 took almost a year to break, though I won't keep Dinah that long. It will be impossible to, though I would love the opportunity to dig into her mind, undisturbed and left to my almost-unlimited well of resources, for that length of time.

The pen tip tears the page a little, and I realize I am gripping it too hard, a side effect of my anger, which is still at a boiling point despite the hours that have passed since I realized her deceit.

I force myself to set down the writing utensil and lace my hands over the top of my head. Leaning back in my seat, I stretch the muscles in my chest and give my emotion a moment to dispel.

Emotion, in any situation, is unproductive. Often, it can be destructive, and that is what I am trying to avoid. I will need to handle this very carefully. Dinah is a woman who will be missed, one with a family that will be a big problem for me if not headed off at the pass.

I will have to be smart, but that doesn't mean I can't enjoy this process while I make the proper arrangements.

I move my attention to my desk calendar and pencil in a session at 3:00 p.m. A joint session, which will be my first.

I stand and grab my jacket and my briefcase. I need to hurry if I'm going to make it to the campus in time for my class.

I open the office door, and her screams grow louder.

CHAPTER 57

DINAH

I ignore the smoothies, even though my mouth tastes like bitter cotton. I know what he puts in there—a cocktail of antidepressants and mood-altering meds—and I have to be sharp for whatever comes.

I really need to know what time it is. I understand why there isn't a clock in here, given that Melonie lost that privilege a few weeks back, but since I have the appointment at eleven thirty with the union rep, it's driving me crazy to not have any sense of bearing.

I've probably already missed it. I picture Natalie getting the call, her dark-brown forehead wrinkling as she gets the news. She'll call me, then immediately follow up the call with a text.

This is inexcusable, Dinah.

Call me immediately, Dinah.

She loves to use my name. It's a control mechanism for her, a way to point out that she is my superior, despite the fact that we went through the training academy together and that bitch scored lower than I did in every single aptitude test except for kissing ass.

He took my cell phone when he put me in here. My cell and his. I didn't even have time to go through his, to do my bimonthly sweep to see what my husband has been up to. Maybe it is clean, his normal back-and-forth volleys with his few male friends and colleagues. Joe is selective about his circle and is most verbose with me. Once, I found a message thread with my mother, a fairly long conversation about what to do for my fortieth birthday. In it, he told her that I was the love of his life. Even though I knew that, the confession still gave me a spike of pleasure; there is something about a man's public profession of love that is incredibly sexy.

I am the love of his life, yet he put me in here. Put an IV in the back of my hand, drugged me, and left me alone all night. It's the first night we've spent apart in years. The last time was when Sal's girlfriend had her baby, an emergency C-section that went wrong. When her contractions began, I flew to Las Vegas to be at her bedside and was the lone representative of our family.

No one should have a baby alone. I told Sal that it was too traumatic of an event, that she needed to have some support. He was in the midst of a trial, had promised to come the following day, didn't see the urgency that I did. I had my own cases, my own appointments, but I dropped them all and arrived just twenty minutes before the baby went into fetal distress and an emergency C-section was ordered.

Alyssa needed someone; she clung to my hand as if it were a life preserver and whispered through her tears that she was terrified. That if something happened, to tell her baby that she loved her. By the time Sal arrived, both mother and daughter had made it through, and he swept in the door with flowers and a big smile, unaware of the risks she'd just overcome. She hugged him, and over his shoulder, our eyes met in silent solidarity.

The door to the room clicks open, and I whirl around to see Joe step in, clipboard in hand, his lab coat on. That stupid coat. A costume, designed to invoke respect and authority. If someone in a white lab coat gives you a pill, you take it. If they tell you something is wrong with you, you believe it. It's the basis of Joe's entire research—the power of suggestion and influence. A lab coat is the anthesis of that.

I don't rush to him, despite the desire. I've had hours to consider my strategy, and begging and pleading with him won't work. No, this battle will be won the same way our courtship happened: reluctant participation.

My husband loves a puzzle, not a path.

"Hello, Dinah."

"I have an appointment with the union rep today at eleven thirty. It's very important. If you want to keep me here, fine, but take me to it and then bring me back. I can't miss it. I'll be fired."

"So be fired." He pulls a pen from the pocket of his coat and writes something on his clipboard, and if it was possible for me to hit a new level of irritation, he just got me there. "You don't need the job. In fact, right now would be a good time to pen your resignation letter."

I know this cold delivery, the flat press of his mouth. He's mad at me.

"I can't do that." I knot my arms over my chest and wonder how long it will be before he brings me something else to wear. At what point he'll allow soap and shampoo and a towel. In this place, everything is a gift and up to him to grant.

"Sure you can. It's not like we need the money." He shrugs, and I don't like the reference. Yes, he has money. Insane piles of it. It's always been a quiet part of our life. I have access to it if I need it; we use it when there's a reason to but ignore it the rest of the time.

"It's not the money." I inhale. If there's a time to tell him, it's now. "I'm being investigated by Internal Affairs. That's what today's meeting is about. If I quit, I'll look guilty, and it won't stop the investigation. If anything, it will heighten it."

He pauses, then puts the pen in the clip at the top of the board, and finally, I have his full attention. "Explain."

"Explain what?"

"Explain what the *fuck* Internal Affairs is investigating." His tone is dark. This is the version of my husband that I respect and fear the most.

"I don't know." I square my shoulders and keep my voice strong and competent. "I was hoping to find out something today."

"You've kept this a secret from me." He closes the distance between us and stops when he is less than a foot away. He's wearing the gray pin-striped suit, which means he went home before his class and changed. Did he water the plants? Drag the trash cans to the curb? Did he take his allergy medicine and his supplements? Normally, I put them out each morning, a neat little line of vitamins and pills, followed by a glass of water. I always clean out the Excursion after our weekends, which he follows up with an Armor All wipe down and vacuum. Had that been done? How many degrees is our axis off by?

I swallow the questions and look up into his face. "I wasn't sure how big of a deal it was. I was assessing and collecting information."

His hand closes on my throat, and it's so big it covers my entire stretch of neck cords. His fingers wrap around, almost touching together on the nape of my neck. It is comforting, the grip—any fear held at bay by the absolute confidence that my husband will not physically hurt me. "You're lying to me, Dinah."

I stare into his eyes and tell him the truth. "I didn't want to bring it to you unless I knew how serious it was or wasn't."

"Which cases are they looking into?"

"I don't know yet. Lacey Deltour. Riley Biff. Maybe more. They had someone following up on my investigation of Reese and Jessica to make sure I was doing my job."

He says nothing, and I know this look on his face. He's thinking. Judging. Calculating. He releases my neck and turns away. "You already missed that meeting, so we'll deal with that after your session."

"I'm not doing a session." I speak before I have time to think, and it's a mistake, defying him right now.

He pauses, and when he turns around, his face is set, his eyes cold, and when he speaks, his voice is steel, each word a knife stabbing deeper. "You are a patient, Dinah. You are not special. You do not have your own unique set of rules. You obey the guidelines you are given, or you will be released. If you think I won't do it, talk back to me again and spend tonight in the box."

I pin my lips together. I have only a few fears in life. The box is one of them.

CHAPTER 58

DINAH

I am intimately familiar with handcuffs but have never had them around my own wrists, not in the last fifteen years. The last time was during the police academy, when we practiced cuffing and uncuffing suspects until it was a second-nature action we could do in the dark.

Having the metal cinched around my own wrists, no key in sight, my wrists pinned to either arm of the chair in front of Joe's desk, is an entirely different feeling. They are unnecessarily tight, pinching the skin in an uncomfortable manner. I shift in the seat, trying to adjust to a better position, but it doesn't help.

I twist my head, trying to see the door to the office and where Joe went, but I swear he intentionally put this chair in a position to block my view. A power move. It doesn't surprise me, and isn't necessary. I will do what he says and I will say the same thing, no matter how much psychological warfare he employs.

His footsteps sound, and I stiffen at the realization that there are two sets of footfalls. There's only one person he might bring in here, so I am unsurprised when he journeys around the edge of the desk and has Jessica with him.

"Dinah, you've already met Jessica." He gestures for her to take a seat. She is not cuffed, and a sharp pain of jealousy stabs at me. There is no one on this earth he trusts more than me, yet I am tied down like a dog while she is free. Why? How? I glare at him, and he smiles. This is intentional. Another power move. He's embarrassing me. I would have thought we were above this, but apparently, it's this easy to puncture our balloon of respect.

"Hi," she says, almost shyly.

I don't respond. The one thing this isn't going to be is a friendship-building exercise. I glance at her left wrist, which has a fresh bandage, and envision him bent over her, his touch gentle. I press my lips together and look away.

With all my mental preparation for a conversation with Joe, I did not prepare for a face-to-face with her. Joe never commingles his patients. Great lengths are taken to make sure they are siloed and independent from each other. Communication in a facility like this will lead to mutiny. It is the job of the facility—our job—to keep the ship steady and head off potential problems.

I am a potential problem. It is a risk for Joe to have me in this close proximity to her. It only makes sense if he trusts me to keep my mouth shut, and that trust warms my soul. I need that hit, and I inhale deeply, reminding myself that today is a hiccup. That's all.

"Jessica, are you curious about why Dinah is being restrained?"

"Yeah, it seems kind of strange." Her voice is quiet, and I'm curious at how drugged up she is and how much of this she will remember. More important, how much of the past she is aware of right now. I have a feeling this session is going to be an inquisition, one designed to find out what secrets I am keeping.

"Dinah, why don't you tell Jessica why you came into her room?"

I hate the tone he's using. It's that mild, passive-aggressive manner he learned from watching *Dr. Phil* on repeat. Even the way he's sitting right now—his chair pulled to the side of his desk so that we are in a small half circle, his ankle resting on his opposite knee, his hands clasped on top of his lap, elbows jutting out as if he's an altar boy.

I clear my throat. "I came into your room to try to kill you." I glare at my husband and am rewarded with a small crook of his lips. That response, he wasn't expecting. I'm sure his normal patients hem and haw and make excuses, but if I want him to believe my lies, I need to be brutal with my truths.

I look away from Joe and look to Jessica. "I was going to cut your wrists and stage it to look like a suicide."

Her eyes widen, but she really shouldn't be surprised by anything at this point.

CHAPTER 59

JESSICA

God, this bitch is crazy. How do they even let her work in a place like this? No wonder he cuffed her to the chair. No wonder she and Mom don't talk. I always wondered how anyone could not get along with Mom. I mean, she's like the chillest person in the world.

"Jessica? How do you feel, hearing that?"

What a dumb question. I must look at him in a way that conveys that, because he chuckles and holds up his hand as if to cancel the question. Thank God, because I really wasn't sure what to say. *Ummm . . . not good?*

"Let me rephrase the question: Why do you think Dinah wanted to kill you?"

"Because she's nuts?" That seems pretty obvious to me. "I mean, no offense."

"I'm talking about more of a personal motivation." He leans forward as if he's really curious about what I'm about to say.

I hate to break it to him, but I have no idea why a woman I've never met before hates me to the point of trying to fake my suicide. I shrug and he seems disappointed by the response.

"Joe, I'm not sure that this is—"

"Shut up, Dinah," he says smoothly, and she flinches like he just slapped her. I look down at my legs. Damn, this is awkward. I hope he doesn't speak to me like that.

"Jessica, I'm thinking that Dinah wanted to kill you for a different reason." His leg bounces for a moment; then he swings it off his knee and leans forward, resting both forearms on his thighs.

"What's that?" I ask.

"Joe—" Dinah says faintly.

"Yes?" He turns to her. "I'd love to hear your input on this. Would you like to share? But be aware . . ." He leans in until their faces are just a foot apart. "Lie about it, and I'll put you in the box."

Her face goes white and I straighten up, alarmed.

"What's the box?"

They both ignore me. They are just staring at each other as if they are communicating with their minds.

"What's in the box?" I repeat, louder.

"I don't know why I did it," she says quietly. "It was a mistake, Joe. I . . ." She tries to reach for him, but the handcuffs keep her arms in place. Frustrated, she screams, her muscles straining as she tries to force the movement. Only her legs are free, and her tennis shoes skid across the wood as she bucks in place. "I'm sorry," she sobs, and starts to cry big gulping tears, like that kid I used to babysit across the street.

"It's okay," I say awkwardly. "I mean, you *did* stop."

"I know exactly why you won't tell me, Dinah." He grips her chin and lifts it until their eyes are level. "It's because you're afraid of losing me. But I already know the truth. So I'm going to need to hear it from you or else you're going to go in the box."

"What's the box?" I ask again, and I'm not sure why I'm even in here, since this seems to be some personal problem between the two of them. To be honest, it's super awkward. Granted, I'm not in a hurry to go back to my room. Even waist deep in tension, it's better than just staring at the walls, wearing a diaper. He gave me a clean pair of scrubs for this. I mean, it's not my best color—salmon—but he traded the diapers for a pair of clean underwear, which is like, heaven. And he said I've been really good and am going to be moved to a different room with a toilet and get fresh clothes each morning.

So, whatever. I'll sit here while they stare into each other's eyes and talk like the end of the world is about to happen. Honestly, I don't really care why my crazy aunt wanted to kill me. Just fire her or arrest her or whatever, and get on to mealtime. I haven't been fed all day. I almost said something when he came into my room earlier, but I figured we were going into a session and I could just ask him in the session, and then she was here and now it seems like it will be rude to bring it up while she's all teary and shit.

"Okay," she sniffs, and he carefully wipes his thumbs under her eyes, getting the tears. She sobs, her gaze stuck to him, and the sound is the same as when my vacuum cleaner whines. Like a long, stretched-out cry. Total drama queen. "I didn't want you to ever find out about her."

I got news for this bitch. He knew about me before she went Edward Scissorhands on my wrists. I was his patient. We've spent like a week together. Talk about beating a dead horse.

"What's special about her? Why would it matter if I found out about her?" He asks the question in the way someone who already knows the answer would, and I tune back in to the conversation. I've been described as a lot of things, but *special* was never one of them.

She pauses, and her face crumples in the moment before she speaks. "Because she's my daughter."

CHAPTER 60

JOE

I already know the truth, but it is still difficult to hear it from her lips. Not because of the situation, but rather the decade of lies behind it.

My wife has a daughter. In all our conversations about children and our future, she has been in staunch agreement with me on the benefits of a two-person household. We've discussed other couples, our opinions of their decisions made and the consequences of such, and we've always been, at least in my mind, a united front. She's had thousands of opportunities to tell me about a child, a baby who is now an adult, and she has intentionally, over and over again, lied by omission, if not outright deceit.

"You understand how this confuses me," I say evenly, as if the anger isn't swelling through every blood vessel in my body. "Because it has always been my understanding that you are a virgin."

Another lie. Not as painful as the first, but still one that burns hot through my veins. It was another way we were in sync—both of us uninterested in human flesh, in the ridiculous act of copulation, one that has little to no benefits but dozens of risks. It was a badge of honor that I carried, one that underlined my ability to trust her implicitly with other men. I was the only one she lusted for, and she did so with a level of decorum and distance that pleased me. Pleased *us*.

But look, another lie.

"It was horrible," she says quietly. "I didn't know him. He forced himself on me and held me down."

If that is meant to evoke sympathy, it doesn't. A traumatic experience in her youth? This would have been a gold mine of discovery, an exploratory event that could have brought us closer to each other and given me mountains of information about my wife. Instead, it is another stab in the fabric of our bond. At this rate, our marriage is a pincushion.

"Wait a minute." Jessica speaks up, and I forgot that my little pawn was still in the room. "You're not my mom."

"Disappointed?" I say crisply. "I understand why."

Dinah's features collapse in response.

"Um, that's a little harsh," Jessica says meekly. "But, uh—no. She's my aunt." She points to Dinah, and she looks as confused as I initially did. "I told you that."

Dinah's gaze flicks back to me, and she ignores Jessica's statement. "She doesn't matter. It's nothing. It was over twenty years ago, and I locked it away and pretended it never happened. I meant everything I said to you, from the moment I met you."

"And your mother?" I tilt my head. "She knows, right?"

She sighs. "Yes. No one else in my family does. I was sent away for the pregnancy. Mom told them I needed therapy."

So many moments with her mother. So many times I spoke of my wife as if I knew her intimately. So many instances where I looked like an absolute idiot.

The rage, which has been simmering at a greater and greater temperature as I wade deeper into her lies, boils over, and I whip my hand out and slap Dinah across the face. The connection of my palm and her cheek is loud, and Jessica shrieks in surprise. It is hard, so much so that I feel the movement of her bones, my palm smarting from the action. When she brings her face forward, a dark-red drop of blood appears at her nostril.

She does not cry, she does not beg. She stares at me, defiant.

This is the version of the woman I fell in love with.

Too bad some loves aren't built to last.

CHAPTER 61

JESSICA

I don't know what the fuck is going on, but I feel like I'm in some episode of *Black Mirror* or something. Dr. Joe just pimp-slapped his nurse, who is handcuffed to the chair and supposedly tried to kill me last night and is also claiming to be my mom? Maybe I'm hallucinating all this, because this is like the craziest soap opera episode ever.

Whatever is going on, I'm done. Like, jail might actually be better than this. Especially if slapping people is okay. There seems to be no oversight in this place. Are there any other doctors? Can I be transferred? Can I complain to a manager? I mean, the fact that I'm grateful for underwear is ridiculous.

He's up in her face right now, ranting at her, and there's definitely some personal drama at work here. I inch to the edge of my seat and jump in as soon as he pauses to take a breath. "Um, excuse me?"

"What?" he bites out, but he isn't looking at me. He's locked in on her, and he looks super pissed. And I was thinking about *marrying* a guy like him. See, that's why I can't find love. I pick assholes. Assholes dressed up to look like sweethearts.

"I have to go to the bathroom," I say quietly.

"Hold it."

"But I can see the bathroom like, right there. Is it okay if I go real quick?" I point to the open door; it's literally five steps away.

"No."

This is ridiculous. "I'll be like two minutes. I promise." I'm great at this. Mom says I could wear down a pencil eraser just from asking it to death.

"Think about our life together," she says quietly. "Think about your proposal. Your—"

"You guys keep talking; I'll be right back," I whisper, and I stand, easing around his chair. He looks at me, then at the open door, the bathroom sign half-visible.

"Be quick," he orders. "Then right back here."

"I will," I promise. I move fast, before he changes his mind, easing through the open door and pushing open the swing door into the bathroom. There are two stalls, and I use the first one, sighing in relief at the gush of urine.

I'm so lucky I haven't gotten a UTI. I've had two so far this year, which supposedly means I'm chronic. Talk about the worst pain of my life. Pissing wasn't even the worst part, even though it felt like razors coming out.

I wipe and pull up the cotton underwear and scrub pants, tightening the drawstring and tying it into a bow. I wash my hands, taking my time with the soap and doing the full twenty-second process that Chunky Mike's always stipulates but we never actually do, scrubbing the soap underneath my fingernails and over my palms before I rinse them clean. I grab two paper towels and pat my hands dry, then smell them. Lavender, and maybe vanilla? Super yummy. I push on the door and peek out.

Their voices are quiet, and now he's got a hand on both of her chair's armrests, pinning her wrists down as she says something. It sounds like she is crying, and I hesitate, not thrilled at the prospect of returning. I glance down the hall, and at the end of it is a door with a wide bar instead of a knob. Not a closet. An exit.

Maybe I could just leave.

I hesitate, then step in that direction, moving down the hall and toward the door at the end. *Lie about it, and I'll put you in the box.*

I was going to cut your wrists and stage it to look like a suicide.

I mean, how many red flags do I need? What is the worst-case scenario if I leave? I already supposedly killed my mom. Playing hooky from psychotherapy has to be a slap on the wrist compared to that.

I take a few more steps away from his office, listening to see if he notices. He doesn't, and I move faster, breaking into a jog as I get farther down the hall. My socks are silent on the tile floor, the anti-slip pattern on the bottom helping me gain traction.

There's a cry from one of the rooms to my left, and I pause at the sound. The hall is empty, and for the first time, I really study the place. It's all glistening white walls and tile floors. The room beside me has *Higgins* written in neat Magic Marker on a label on the door.

There's another cry from inside the room, and I reach for the door handle and pause again, unsure if I should open it. Maybe there's a psychopath in there, one who used to eat people on the weekends.

Fuck it. I turn the handle and pull.

Well, that's anticlimactic. It doesn't budge.

The room has the same little door thing that the food comes through, and I crouch down and flip the lock, then swing open the door.

There's a woman's face right there, and I fall backward, clamping my hand over my mouth to stop the scream. She's old, like my mom's age, and her eyes dart to the left and the right like Ping-Pong balls. "Who are you?" she whispers, and her voice sounds like cheese coming through the grater.

Her breath is terrible; I'm five feet away, and it's like a hand, covering my face, refusing to let me breathe. Is mine that bad? I try to remember brushing my teeth, and it has been a bit. "I'm Jessica—"

"You gotta get me out of here," she hisses. "My name is Tricia Higgins. I have two children. Call the police. Have you called the police?"

"No, I—" I look back at Dr. Joe's office.

"Go get help," she says urgently, her hand gripping the opening. Her fingernails are all bitten to the quick. "Hurry. Before they find you."

I push up to my feet and don't wait for more. I'm four steps from the exit, and I hit the bar with both hands and it gives, the metal door swinging open. No alarm sounds, and I spill out, then stop in the bright afternoon sun.

I'm in the woods.

It's such a surprise that I take a moment and stare, not understanding what I'm seeing. I had been expecting a view of Pomona Avenue or perhaps a back parking lot. Instead, there's pine straw everywhere and an older SUV parked next to a tree stump. From somewhere to my left, a bird chirps. I whirl around, and the building before me looks like an old barn, the stall doors boarded up. Had I not just come out of it, I would have called it abandoned. I look back at the door I came out of, and there's a small keypad hidden beside the handle, the only hint of what is inside.

This feels bad. Like, really bad. I stumble backward, then turn and consider my options. There's a wide road that goes off through the woods. I head toward it, breaking into a run on the soft pine straw.

CHAPTER 62

DINAH

I don't know how to fix this. The look in his eyes . . . it isn't a part of my husband I've ever seen. This isn't Joe. This is a man without a soul, one fueled by rage and hurt. I did that to him. I pushed him to this place, one where he screams at me as if I am a misbehaving child. My cheek is still stinging from his slap. For a decade, he's never so much as grabbed me too tightly, much less put his hands on me like that.

I may have misjudged my husband, and discovering that while you are handcuffed to a chair is far from ideal. Throughout all my years searching for and researching missing and dead women, there have been countless times where I have scoffed at their stupidity. For staying with an abusive partner, for choosing a high-risk path when there were safer options, for not seeing a murderer until they had their knife in her gut.

All that time on the intellectual high road, and yet here I am, a prisoner stupid enough to think I can sweet-talk my way out of this. Maybe I can. But maybe I can't. I need a plan B, just in case.

"I know you're mad at me," I say quietly, hoping to lower the volume of his emotion. "But we can fight about this after we figure out how to get me back to the station before Natalie raises the alarm."

"Fuck Natalie," he says, and a bit of his spittle lands on my cheek.

"If we fuck Natalie, we fuck everything we've built," I say evenly. He might be crazy right now, but he is not stupid. Implementation plans and cover stories are his specialty, building narratives and red herrings his favorite hobby, followed closely by the anticipation and advance solving of problems. "This isn't a coworker; this is the chief of the LAPD, Joe." I will him to think, to understand what I'm saying. I don't know where my soulmate is, but he has to come up for breath at some point.

"Why didn't you tell me when we met?" he asks, and there's a fracture in his voice, a crack in the anger, one that reveals the deep pool of hurt underneath.

Because I would have looked like damaged goods. It's the truth that I can't admit. My pride is too great for that. Not just my pride—my fear. My fear that saying it will cause it to become true. Maybe he already sees me as that, but if not now, putting that thought into his head will cause it to stick. I'd rather him be mad at me over uninterested. I've always been a prize in his eyes. To fall from that height might kill me.

"Answer me," he grits out, and when he pushes off my wrists, it feels like the small bones in the left one crack. I yelp, but he doesn't react, crossing his arms in front of him and waiting for a response.

Why didn't you tell me when we met? I try to think of a response, something he will believe and accept. I glance toward the bathroom, not wanting Jessica to come in during this, the embarrassment already unbearable.

"I was so young when it happened," I say softly. "I was only sixteen. By the time I met you a decade later, I just . . . It didn't even seem real to me. It was something I had buried so deep that it was like it didn't happen."

I have and had tried so hard to forget it. I've tried but failed. It is impossible when the reminders are everywhere, a memory I can't run away from.

Jessica was ten when I met Joe. Had she been in my life, he never would have dated me. Never would have chased me. Never would have fallen for me, or proposed, or become the second part of my soul.

She would have taken that away from me.

Would she do it to me now?

"Don't let this destroy us," I whisper. It's a fight not to say it without crying. "I was trying to kill her to protect us. You don't have to wonder where my priorities are. She won't affect us. Nothing has to change."

He stares at me, his face stony, but I can see the wheels turning in his mind.

CHAPTER 63

JOE

Nothing has to change.

I've always prided myself on seeing through any deception my wife has tried to slip past me. All that bravado, and all complete bullshit. I don't know this woman at all.

When she brought up the latest candidate for the clinic, I didn't sense I was a pawn. When we planned and researched and prepared, I didn't see a single red flag. We had dozens of different conversations and strategy sessions, all designed to think through any risk and cover any possible contingency plan. Hundreds of points where I should have picked up on the fact that she had an ulterior motive.

I missed it all. If I'm that blind to her scheming, how can I trust her in the future? I'm now second-guessing my ability to judge anyone anymore. For a psychologist, self-doubt is the kiss of death, and she just gave me that Achilles' heel.

Thank you, dear wife. You are the gift that keeps on giving, one I am beginning to regret purchasing.

Don't let this destroy us.

Will it? I don't know, but the good news is, I don't have to decide that right now. All I have to decide is how to handle the damage control with the outside world.

She's a patient now, which means I can take my time with her. Between my mental manipulations and the box, I'll find out everything I want to know.

CHAPTER 64

JESSICA

My left sock has ripped, my heel now exposed and bleeding. Every step is painful, and my right foot isn't much better. Between the state of my feet and the wheeze of my chest, I need to walk, but I'm too afraid to.

My initial thought—that I'd get in trouble for checking myself out—is gone, because whatever that place is, it's not legit. I'm not even sure it's legal. Unless it's some government black ops site—and why would *I* be at a black ops site?

It doesn't make sense. None of it. And now, I'm starting to think through everything I should have questioned. Like why I wasn't being arrested for what I supposedly did to my mom. Was that bullshit too? Probably. I just need my brain to be clear. I'm a smart girl when I'm not in some medication-induced fog. My mom used to always say that. *So much smarter than me!* She said it so much that I asked once if I got my brains from my dad. That, apparently, hadn't been the smart thing to ask. She got really quiet, and I felt like an asshole, and I know you're not supposed to speak ill of the dead, but I was paying him a compliment, sort of, so it seems like it would have been okay.

Someone's got to drive down this road at some point. It's not overgrown at all, so someone is using it a lot. There's like, nothing out here.

A bunch of trees and a fence. I haven't seen anything since I left that building—not even a mailbox or power line.

I look back. The road has curved, the building now hidden from view. I don't know if they're chasing me or not. If not yet, they will be. He seems like he'd be fast, probably runs marathons on the weekends and shit. The only time I run is to the couch if a new episode of reality TV is on. Other than that, the last time I did any version of cardio was when I tried to be on top during sex and had to switch positions after thirty seconds because my thighs gave out.

A tight pain in my rib cage hits, and I stumble to a walk and press my hand against the cramp, attempting to massage out the knot. I look back and speed walk, scanning the sides of the path. If I hear an engine, I'll sprint into the trees and hide. He won't know where I left the path. The straw will hide any footprints—not that I'll leave any in my socks. There's a bend ahead, and it looks like a clearing. I force myself to jog again, wincing with each step.

At the clearing, I can stop. Maybe there will be a gas station or a neighborhood. A river. I would kill for something to drink.

Ten more steps. I count them down, my lungs protesting as I push my body to its limit.

I fall short. It takes another few footfalls, but then I am at the clearing, and I stop, because here the road ends, the path branching off to the left and the right to make way for a pasture. And there, way across the pasture, I see a house, one with an honest-to-God white picket fence and flowers in the window boxes and some wind chimes swinging off the porch. I duck under the fence rail and start to run toward it. The grass is soft, and even my cramp is on board, softening as I sprint toward freedom.

CHAPTER 65

DINAH

Joe crosses his arms over his chest and walks in a small circle, his chin down, as if he is thinking, and when he faces me, there's a slight smile on his face. "I think . . . ," he says slowly, then pauses. "Do you know what I think, Dinah?"

He's torturing me. That's what this is. He knows that right now I'm hanging on every word, desperate for his forgiveness and approval. He's not going to give it to me, even if he's ready for it. He's going to stretch this out for as long as he can. Not just hours. Days. Maybe weeks.

And I won't be rescued. Tonight, he'll create a plan, one that will require my cooperation, and of course I'll give it. I'll give it because it will be a stipulation, a requirement that I'll have to satisfy in order to get his warmth, his time, or any number of other things. Water. Food. Air. I think of the box, and an involuntary shudder rips through me. When he built the box, it was the first time I voiced any opposition. I thought it was too cruel. Too intense. He countered my concerns by saying it was the extremity of the treatment that would cause it to be so effective. And he has been right so far. The patients will say whatever he wants after a few hours in there. If they don't, then they stay in longer. Becca lasted two days. I don't know how she did it, but she was the first one he released. Probably because she was such a black mark in his files.

By the time he lets me out, I won't have a job. I might not have a husband. Whatever the outcome, he'll be unscathed. Joe always comes out on top. He has his whole life. Our entire marriage. His—

"Answer me."

I can't remember the question. Oh, if I know what he thinks. "No," I say quietly. He's already breaking me down. I've been so stupid in our marriage, thinking that we were equals. Thinking that I had a voice and an opinion and strength.

"I think . . ." He pauses, looking toward the bathroom. His gaze sharpens, and whatever he was about to say is gone. "I think Jessica has been in the bathroom too long."

I try to look over my shoulder, to follow his movement as he goes to the door, but I can't. I listen, hearing his dress shoes click down the hall and into the bathroom, then back out. When he reappears, his face is tight with worry. "She's not there." He yanks his hand into his pocket and pulls out his keys, flipping through them until he gets to the handcuff key.

"Just go," I urge. "I can wait here." I could escape here, left alone in this office. I could break this chair and get free. Find something to pick the handcuff lock.

He shakes his head. Of course my husband wouldn't be that dumb. He frees one hand, then the other, before roughly grabbing my arms and pushing me through the door and to the closest room. Jessica's.

"Joe," I protest, struggling against him as he unlocks the door, "I can help you catch her. Let me help."

"Get in. I'll be back." He shoves me into the room, the unlocked handcuffs still hanging from my wrists, and slams the door. I make it back just in time to see the dead bolt cylinder lock into place. I pound the metal with the side of my fist, and the cuffs clang loudly against it. "Joe!" I call out. "Let me help!"

I put my ear to the door but can't hear anything through the thick metal.

CHAPTER 66

JESSICA

My legs give out as I make it to the house's yard. I wobble across the neatly cut grass and up the front porch steps. The front door is bright red, and I press the doorbell, then use the knocker. I wait a minute, then try again.

"Come on . . . ," I mutter, and move to the window, cupping my hands and peering in. It's hard to see, but it's dark inside. No sign of movement.

I walk to the edge of the porch and lean over the railing, trying to see if there's a car parked around the side of the house. There's a detached garage there, but it looks like the type people store other stuff in instead of vehicles. On the edge of the garage is a light pole and a line that runs from it to the house. I study it, then look up at the rest of the lines running to the house. They go off to the left, following the driveway, and I'm assuming to a road, one with actual pavement and cars.

Maybe one of these wires is for a telephone. I ring the doorbell again and then put my hand on the knob, turning it slightly, just to test it. It turns and the door cracks open. Surprised, I stare at the crack, then look around, double-checking that I'm all by myself.

"Hello?" I call out, putting my mouth to the crack. "Is anyone home?" I ease the door open. Inside, it's super cute, like a cozy-library-meets-woodsy-lodge feel. There's got to be a phone in here. If not a phone, then at least a pair of shoes. "Hello?" I belt out the greeting as loudly as I can as I step in. I can't believe this place is unlocked. Mom always preached the "every lock, every time" philosophy, and had convinced me at an early age that if you leave your shit unattended, someone will help themselves to it.

Five minutes, max. I'll look for a phone and a pair of shoes. Quick in and out before the owners come back and think I'm an intruder.

I close the door behind me, then pause, looking down at the smooth, polished floor. My socks are disgusting and wet. I hold on to the wall and peel off my socks, then hiss at the cut on the bottom of my right foot. I'll look for some hydrogen peroxide and a Band-Aid.

I leave the socks on the interior welcome mat and wipe my bare feet carefully, then move forward.

The living room is open to the kitchen, which has one of the green stoves that my favorite internet chef has. I scan the counters, looking for a phone cradle, but there's nothing there. I open the first door I come to—a small bathroom. The next door is a bedroom with two double beds. There are personal items on the bedside tables and an open door that gives a glimpse into a large bath. Scanning the dresser for a phone, I come up short. A woman's watch. Perfume bottle. Brush and discarded shirt. A novel. I keep moving into the bathroom and start opening drawers, looking for first aid supplies.

The third drawer has a pharmacy's worth of items, and I grab hydrogen peroxide and some antibiotic ointment. I prop my right foot up on the edge of the sink and carefully pour the brown bottle over the wound. It foams up, and I set down the bottle and wait a moment, letting it work. There's a silver frame facing the other sink, and I hop a little to the left and position it toward me so I can see.

It's Dr. Joe and the nurse.

I stare at it in horror. I pull my foot from the sink and do a slow turn, trying to find any other clues as to the homeowners. A woman's robe hanging from the hook. I reopen the drawers and grab the men's cologne, lifting it to my nose.

It's his. The expensive scent hits my nose, and I recoil at it. Shit. I need to get out of here. I grab the box of assorted Band-Aids, and they spill. Picking up one of the larger sizes, I pause at the sound of a door slamming and the creak of the wood floor.

Someone is here.

CHAPTER 67

JOE

I've never felt so alive. Maybe this is why lords hunt foxes. There was that novel, decades back, where the victims were released and the teams took up chase. It's exhilarating, the thought that my little patient is on the run, her heart beating fast inside that young chest, her adrenaline pushing her to keep going despite the fatigue her muscles must be facing.

She's not the first to escape. The last was a patient for over four years. Her muscles had atrophied, her health was poor, and I caught her easily, on the ridge, just a quarter-mile from the road. It was a close enough call for us to install the fencing, which is why I'm not too concerned about this little event. Had she taken the Excursion, it would be cause for alarm. But I have the key to that in my pocket, and on foot, she would never make it. She might make it to one of the fences. But try to crawl over them, and she'd be hit with five thousand volts of electricity. Not enough to kill, but enough to ensure she wouldn't try again.

I didn't see her on the road from the clinic to the house, so she is likely in the woods. That's fine. I open the coat closet and grab a windbreaker, the thick one, which will protect me from the branches and thorns of the forest. Tossing it on the couch, I shed my suit jacket and stop at the fridge to grab a bottled water.

Maybe she'll change her mind and come back to the clinic. I'll pull up and see her huddled outside the door, her face apologetic, her arms scratched up, feet bloody. She'll beg forgiveness and I'll grant her some initial mercy.

From that moment, though, our relationship will have changed. Dinah has ruined this one for me. I chug the water and think about all the wasted hours, all my notes and plans. Jessica was so close to breaking. Today, in fact, probably would have been her moment. *Yes, I killed my mother. I remember it. I remember why I did it.*

It would have been beautiful. Glorious. And now it's gone.

I take in the last drop and crumple the water bottle in my fist, then open the drawer to the trash can and chuck it in. Reaching up, I undo the top button of my dress shirt, then begin to work my way down. Moving around the island, I head to our bedroom. Another thing that will need to change. No sense in two beds if Dinah will be staying at the clinic. I'll give her the biggest room, of course. She is, at least for now, still my wife. She—

I stop and take a step back, then another, unsure of what I've seen out of the corner of my eye. Retracing my steps into the living room, I peer at the small wet clump on the floor by the front door. It looks like a washcloth. I walk over and bend down, getting a closer look at it.

Wet socks, with the familiar gray pattern of anti-slip tread on the bottom of them.

She's here.

I straighten, my heart beating faster as I absorb the possibilities. I stand and look around the room, gauging the potential hiding spots. Easing around to the left, I check behind the couch and then reopen the coat closet, flicking on the light switch and exploring the small depths.

No twenty-year-old girl. I close the door quietly. So, the bathrooms or bedrooms. I should have visited the garage first and grabbed one of the hunting guns—not that a big weapon is needed with a girl her size. One hard punch would send her to the floor.

Still, I swing by the kitchen and grab my favorite knife from the butcher block, verifying that all the others are there. Maybe she is no longer here, but unless she's an Olympic runner, the timetable makes it likely that she's still in the house. Holding the knife in my right hand, I ease toward the bedrooms. I check the small bathroom first, but the walk-in shower and small space is empty.

Next is our bedroom, and I hesitate in the doorway, aware that if I move inside, she might run from the other room and to freedom. It's a risk I'll have to take, so I step into the room and quickly scan the interior. It looks as it did this morning when I left. Neat and in order. The door to the bathroom is open, but first I crouch and look under Dinah's bed skirt.

A blur of activity happens in my peripheral, and I lift my head up in time to see her streak out from behind my bed and toward the hall. I stick out my foot, and she trips over it, her arms swinging out in an attempt to catch herself, her head banging on the wall with a loud thump. She immediately is in movement, rolling back upward and trying to lunge to her feet, but I tackle her to the floor and straddle her waist.

"Be still," I threaten her, and pick up the knife, which fell in the activity. I bring it to her face and she immediately freezes, her eyes going wide. Funny how so many are so scared of a simple little blade. Is it vanity? Or the fear of a pain they have never experienced? To be honest, the stab doesn't really hurt—not at first. It takes a moment to even realize it has occurred, and then . . . then the pain follows. Like a blood pool spreading faster and faster, the associated pain receptors all coming to life at once. It's fascinating to watch, and each one is different.

"Please," she begs. "Please. Just let me go."

So ungrateful, these patients are. They don't realize that they're making history. Granted, she won't. I might as well cut her throat right now. Not here; that would be too messy. But maybe in the guest-bathroom shower. I consider the distance and the best way to get her there.

"Stay there." I hold the knife against her neck and press on her chest with my other hand, pinning her to the floor as I stand. Straightening, I put my shoe on her sternum and lean on it until she lets out a painful gasp.

She'll walk to her death.

They always do.

CHAPTER 68

DINAH

I stand in the middle of Jessica's room, thinking. Right now, she'd be running. It's a fool's errand, but she doesn't know that. At some point, she'll reach the fences. Unless she's a pole vaulter, she won't be able to get over them without hitting the electric wire. We spent half a million dollars electrifying the land's entire perimeter. The only way in or out is through the driving gate, which is controlled by the remote fobs on our key chains.

Maybe she'll figure something out. She's smart—smart enough to read the room, invent a bathroom need, and take off running. I didn't suspect anything, mostly because I was frantically trying to save my marriage. Joe and I were both distracted over the issue, which is the only reason she found that opening.

There have been a few rare moments in the last twenty years when I have mourned the baby I gave away. *I loved her.* That's something I never told anyone, something I will never confess to Joe, no matter how long he locks me in the box for—but after her birth, the nurses wrapped her in a lilac towel and put her in my arms, and I started to cry because she was so perfect and so vulnerable and mine. The only thing I had ever created, and the love was so scary, so big and fierce and bold, that I couldn't take it. I sobbed and I hugged her close and I pressed kisses all over her face, and then they were taking her away and it felt like my heart left with her.

I locked that part of me away after that. I responded in the immature manner of a sixteen-year-old child. I turned that love into hate and spent the next six weeks in the facility stewing over how unfair my life had become. When the adoption paperwork was delivered, I watched my mother sign it, and another brick was added to the wall around that part of my heart. Years later, when Reese Bishop found me and asked if I wanted to be part of Jessica's life, I signed a new set of papers, ones that guaranteed that Reese would keep my identity from Jessica and that I would never initiate contact or reveal my maternity to her.

Once I met Joe . . . as our relationship progressed . . . I became more and more grateful for that distance, but it would be a lie if I said that I didn't occasionally fantasize about meeting her. Telling her. I've dreamed about her embracing me, us comparing strengths and weaknesses and seeing what hereditary items had passed down, if any.

That joint session made a mockery of that reveal. She didn't even react to the news, other than to call me crazy and tell Joe that it wasn't true. No warm embrace. No forgiveness for abandoning her. None of the different scenarios I had allowed myself to hope for in the rare moments that I indulged in the forbidden fantasy.

Which is fine. I deserve that. I had, after all, just tried to kill her. What had I expected? Her to rush into my arms?

Now she's ruined as a test case for Joe. Her knowing the truth . . . seeing behind Joe's carefully constructed curtain? She'll be useless for his experiments. He will find her, and he will kill her. It's an outcome risk for all the patients, but that's why I've always chosen them so carefully. For the most part, they are women who deserve to be test subjects, if not locked away in prison. The exceptions are the drug addicts or homeless, men and women who have screwed up their lives in unrecoverable ways. The clinic is a kinder place to them than the outside world, assuming they play along with my husband's mental games.

It's not a hard thing to do, yet some of them just can't submit. I don't understand it. If I had Joe's undivided attention for hours at a time, I'd do whatever he wanted—yet they don't. And they wonder why I don't have sympathy for them when they complain.

My stance has always been firm, but now, as a patient with my own file and number, I'm beginning to question my future. I saw the way he looked at me. Pure disgust.

Can you be in love with someone who disgusts you?

Can I be in love with a man who locks me in an electrified box? One that sends an electric current from your toes to your ears at random intervals each hour? One that is so small that you don't have any room to move and barely enough air to breathe? One that is so dark that you have no sense of time or space? Joe designed the box so that the claustrophobia would be at maximum effect, and that when they defecate or urinate, the stench would fill the area. They typically vomit after the first bowel movement, an act that comes quicker due to the electric shocks. The shocks are a laxative of sorts, one that makes the box a shit-filled claustrophobic hellhole where you are constantly steeled against the next volt of electricity, unsure if it is seconds or an hour away.

I've always hated the idea of the box. The rest of it . . . his mad scientist playground where he could conduct his research without the meddlesome oversight of the DHCS or the DSS—that, I understood and supported. The clinic was nice, our secret little world that we reigned over together. It has always been our baby, one that we can leave for a weeklong vacation to France, as long as we put enough supplies in each room for the patient to get by on.

I never, in all the time we spent designing and building the clinic, imagined myself as a patient. On this side of the locked door, it's not nearly as rosy.

I think of everything I do—the cleaning, the smoothie-and-meal preps, the medicine distributions, the laundry, and more. He can't do it all alone; there's too much work, and all things he hates to do. He'll need a nurse, one he can trust, and Joe doesn't trust anyone.

So there's my in, the break that will have to occur in my patient experience. I can barter with it. Negotiate for a better cell. Time with him in his office. Maybe a night away in the ranch house.

I'll need those things. I'll need the special treatment, the reminder of our life together and the love we have. Without it, I won't make it in here. I'm not even sure I'll make it through another session like the one we just had.

That is not the man I love, and this devolution is 100 percent my fault. If being his patient is the punishment for that crime, I accept that but refuse the sentence.

So, how do I get out? I stand in the middle of the room and do a slow turn, thinking through its construction. This room is different from the others. It's the only one without a bathroom, an exclusion due to its interior location being too far from the sewer lines. Joe's office is adjacent to it, at the end, which means that he has skylights and a window. This room has neither. We designed them so that the patients would not have a sense of day or evening, nor any possibility of escape. The ceilings are exposed, and there's no crawl space. The doors are steel; the butler's windows lock from the outside and are too small to crawl through, even if they are left open. A concrete slab is underfoot, and the ductwork is all embedded and too high and too small for access.

But there is one other thing about this room that is unique. I turn and look into the mirror on the wall, which stretches eight feet across and gives Joe a direct look into this room from any location in his office.

I remember when they put this double-sided mirror in. I had smiled at the idea of it, because my husband loves a good cliché, whether or not he realizes he's falling victim to it. So many things here . . . the clipboard he carries, his white lab coats, the formality he uses with his patients . . . they are all things he has seen in movies or during his residency. All adopted to support his ego and vision of this place. The biggest cliché of them all—this window into the room. For observation purposes, he had told me, his chest puffed, face serious.

Sure. Whatever. Another ten-thousand-dollar expense added to the already ridiculous budget. I trimmed costs where I could, downgrading items he wouldn't notice. This two-sided mirror was one of the places where I had found some savings, which is how I know a very important thing that my husband doesn't.

It isn't Teflon, or bulletproof, or double reinforced.

Thank God.

CHAPTER 69

JESSICA

I think he's going to kill me. Honestly. I thought he would take me back, to his office, to my room, to her—but instead, he is pushing me down the hall and toward the small bathroom off the kitchen. I try to dig my heels in to push back, try to twist out of his grip—but he presses the blade of the knife into my neck and I stop.

The blood is already running down my throat, the sharp edge of it nicking me several times in the process. I've stopped begging because that doesn't seem to be working, but I have no idea what else to try.

My mom would know just what to do. Once, when she was in college, she was hijacked and rode in the car for twelve miles with a guy who was high on LSD and had a shotgun pressed into her rib cage. He wanted Dairy Queen, but the DQ in town had closed like six years earlier, and there weren't any others in that town. Somehow, Mom convinced him that a salad would taste just as good and that she made great salads, and got him to agree to stop at a produce stand beside a gas station. When they stopped, she bought two heads of lettuce and some carrots and told the clerk to call the cops, then got back in the car with him.

When I asked her why she got back in, why she didn't just run, she said that then he would have gotten out and probably shot the clerk and anyone else he saw.

She got back in, knowing she might die, and drove him to her apartment, where she fixed him a salad, and was sitting at the table with him, eating, when the cops busted in.

I didn't believe her when she told me that. I didn't believe her for a decade, not until I was doing a history project in eleventh grade and we went to the library and used the microfilm, and I came across an article in the paper with a picture of her holding a head of lettuce, her arm around the store clerk.

I could never have done that. And this, I'm not going to be able to talk my way out of. I'm not her. I don't think quick like that. Maybe I'm not her daughter, after all, and it occurs to me, in the moment before he pushes me into the bathroom and toward the open shower door, that if I'm going to die, I should at least know the truth.

I fall on the white subway tile, my hands catching me, and I look back at Dr. Joe, who is kneeling beside me, his knife in one hand.

"Is she really my mom? That nurse?"

He pauses and wipes his mouth with the back of his knife hand. "Your mom never said anything to you? Anything that might make you think you were adopted?"

Had she? I hold up my hands, showing him my palms. "Let me think a moment. Just, please. Give me a sec."

I try to process twenty years in a few seconds, and come up short. "I mean, my dad is dead. That's what she always said." I think of the photos of him and wonder who that man was, why she had to lie. "And she is kind of old. Older than my friends' moms. But no, she never said anything."

"Lay down on the tile, head toward the drain."

Yeah, that doesn't sound like anything I want to do. I tense and he smiles.

"Don't bother, little lamb. Make one move I don't like, and I'll just start stabbing. This can be quick or it can be painful, so lay down if you want it fast."

The movement is so quick that I don't understand what is happening. A blur above his head. A cracking sound. He tilts forward, and I shriek, diving to one side and hugging the tiled wall as he falls, his knife still stuck out, into the place where I'd been. The nurse—both hands tight around a bronze frog—stands above him, her breath hard, eyes wild.

"The keys are in the Excursion," she gasps. "Head north and use the key fob at the gate."

CHAPTER 70

JESSICA

The Excursion smells like coffee. It bounces over the dirt road and across a cattle gate. When I finally get to a gate, it takes me a full minute to find the clicker, clipped to the visor. I press it and the gate slowly opens. A few minutes later, I reach the paved state road and jam the accelerator down. I inch to the edge of the seat to ease the strain on my short legs, and watch as the speedometer slowly climbs up the dial. It's starting to get dark, and I lean to the left and turn on the headlights.

I can't believe I'm free. My heart beats rapidly, and I force myself to breathe in and out slowly, like Mom taught me to do when I feel like I'm going to have a panic attack. The SUV goes off on the shoulder, shaking violently, and I let off the gas and steer it back onto the road. I'm not really sure I should be driving. I'm definitely impaired, though maybe a cop would give me a pass if they pull me over.

I tap at the display screen, but there's no navigation. Head north, she said. Like I know what direction is north. I do the familiar rhyme—*rises in the east, sets in the west*—and verify that I'm heading to the right of the sunset. North.

The radio is on, and it's playing "Exes" by Tate McRae. I try to picture Dr. Joe bobbing his head to the beat, but I can't. Maybe it's the nurse's playlist.

I'm struck with the memory of her swinging down that frog, right on top of his head. The exhausted victory on her face when he collapsed. That is an image that will stick with me for a while. If she is my mother, it's not a bad image to remember her by.

I didn't lie to Dr. Joe. My mom never said anything that made me suspect adoption. Other than her being old and not wanting to talk about my dead dad, there were no signs. We were just alike, the two of us. Like peas in a pod; she always said that. Once, when I was mad because she wouldn't let me go to Universal Studios on a school night, I told her that we weren't like peas in a pod, that she was stupid and mean and I hated her, and now I wish . . . I wipe at my eyes and slam my hand on the steering wheel and wish more than anything that I could go back in time and take it all back.

She was the greatest mom in the world. The only mom I wanted.

It probably wasn't true, what the nurse—my aunt—said. I mean, these people kept me prisoner in some kind of fake crazy house, then both tried to kill me, so the thing about her being my real mom was probably a lie also. I don't want to be related to that woman back there, even if she did save me at the very last second.

The road curves to the right, and I grip the steering wheel tightly, then let out a shout of joy at what appears around the bend.

A gas station.

CHAPTER 71

DINAH

I didn't plan to help her. I planned to help him hunt her down, but somewhere in between me sneaking into her room to stage her suicide and me walking into our home and hearing her beg my husband for mercy, I grew a conscience.

Maybe it's because when I originally decided to kill her, it was a necessary sacrifice for my marriage—a union I had believed was iron-clad and perfect.

Happy marriages don't end with the wife in a box, begging her husband for mercy. If he could flip on me so easily, I could return the favor and be a good mother for one brief moment in time.

I'll confess, I hit him harder than was necessary. Let's call it me letting off some steam and paying him back for putting me in a cell. It felt good, crashing that bronze frog onto his head. And finally, some use out of the lawn ornament, which had been a birthday present from Sal, a present picked out by his then girlfriend, a finance major with an addiction to online shopping with his credit card.

Honestly, I didn't even need to hit Joe. I had a syringe ready—the same sort he had used on me the night before. But like I said, emotions were running hot and I wanted to tip the power scales back in my favor. So I hit him hard, then carefully injected him with some of the pento.

Just enough to give him a nice little snooze but to make sure he wakes up in time for our departure.

We've discussed our exit plan before and thoroughly prepared for it, because that's what we love to do. My mother once said that our dream date night would just involve a mile-long piece of paper and a pen. She was right, which is why I don't have to wonder what I should do right now.

I know all the steps. What I don't know is how my husband will react when he wakes up, because what I just did—letting a patient out of the clinic—is a situation we've never planned for. It's an unthinkable crime, one worse than me trying to kill one, but not even in the ballpark of me having a secret daughter. If he can forgive me for the latter, then the former won't matter.

I think.

Eventually, he will forgive me for hiding Jessica's existence from him. He'll forgive me for the secret of my lost virginity and any lies I've told him about that. He'll get over that I didn't come to him for help when Reese reached out and told me she was going to tell Jessica all about me.

Reese is the reason this all crashed down. She should have just kept her word, but instead she emailed me, two decades after she took my baby, and requested a lunch. The email was cryptic and short, with an air of urgency that couldn't be ignored.

I ignored it.

Two days later, a second email.

A day later, a call to the station, one they forwarded to my cell.

So I replied to her email and agreed to meet her for lunch. And there, across the white linen tablecloth at Fogarty's, she told me she was going to tell Jessica that I was her real mom. It was not a request for permission; it was a dictation of her plans.

I told her that that was absolutely not okay and against the contract we had agreed to, back when she was a barren woman who was eternally grateful for a child.

She said that she didn't care, that she was dying and didn't want to leave her daughter without a mother.

I sat there, in my blue linen suit, a glass of Diet Coke sweating on the tablecloth, and silently panicked. When the waitress asked for our lunch orders, I requested the check for our drinks. I paid for Reese's tea and went to the restroom, where I had a mini anxiety attack inside one of the stalls.

On my way out, I saw Reese getting into her sedan, and I almost followed her home. I had this wild, impulsive decision to take her right then and deliver her to Joe, but that would have been ridiculous. Reese would have told him everything, and wouldn't have needed any mind tricks or manipulation to do it.

Instead, I waited, and with each day that passed, the chances doubled that she had told Jessica. Each strange number calling my phone filled me with dread. A mosquito-control sprayer knocked on our door one Saturday afternoon and almost gave me a heart attack.

I couldn't live like that. My plan wasn't perfect, I didn't have the time to make it so. Everything was so tight with this one. I had to introduce the idea to Joe and get him to act on it quickly, all before Reese opened her big mouth.

I bought myself a little bit of time. I called Reese and set a second lunch date. Asked her to not tell Jessica until we had a chance to talk. That bought me the ten days I needed, which was the tightest turnaround Joe and I had ever implemented.

I open the closet door, drag over a chair, and stand on it, reaching in for the first of the two suitcases. They are small, just big enough for toiletries and two changes of clothing. We don't need much. At the house in Costa Rica, there are closets stocked full of clothes, fresh linens on the bed, shampoos in the shower, and toothbrushes in their holder. Everything we will need to get started, with Joe's offshore accounts there to fund any and every expense that comes up.

Best of all, a country with no extradition—an important quality, given that Freddie and Natalie will likely figure out all our crimes in short order. All the details I've hidden over the years and the last few days. Things like the coroner's observation that Reese Bishop had never birthed a child. Freddie would love that detail. He'd cackle over all this.

And Joe won't leave me—not right now, with everything in such a precarious state. He might think that he'll leave me later, once we have some distance from all this, but he won't. He'll remember all the things that make us special, and his anger will fade and he'll fall back in love with me.

He will. He has to. I'll take a broken version of us over a life without him.

I walk from the bedroom and toward the half bath, stepping over one of his arms, which is sticking out into the hall. Pausing over him, I pat down his pockets, finding both of our phones and pocketing them. Continuing past him, I open the junk drawer in the kitchen and grab the key fob to the garage. Standing at the window above the sink, I lean forward and click the button to open the large double door.

The movement starts immediately, and I watch as the wide panels lift to reveal the pair of four-wheelers, array of mountain bikes, and then the silver grille of the twenty-year-old Toyota Land Cruiser.

Our getaway vehicle.

CHAPTER 72

JESSICA

"Miss, I'm going to need you to stop crying."

I nod and grab another napkin out of the dispenser that is on the center of the picnic table. Pressing it to my eyes, I try to control the wave of emotion that is pushing up my throat. A sprinkler system—that's what my mom used to call me, and the realization that she'll never call me the nickname again brings a fresh round of tears.

The dam has officially broken. As soon as the officer pulled in and wandered over, all skeptical and wary, it shuddered. When he asked me my name, it cracked. When I told him I thought my mom was dead—that I had seen a police file with her photos—it burst open.

I still don't know, with everything they told me and showed me, if I actually did do something to her. I don't think I did, but I saw those crime scene pictures and the receipt where I bought poison, so maybe I did and he's about to arrest me and take me to jail and whatever. I don't even care, because at least it will be real.

The problem is, I wasn't ready to lose her yet. I had too much I wanted to say, too many questions to ask, and had been writing them all down, asking her a few at a time, spaced out so it wasn't too obvious but also so that I could digest each bite of information before I took the next one. Three months—that's what the doctor had said at her last checkup. She had three months left.

Except now she's gone. And now, with the fog of medicine starting to lift, it's like all the emotions have hit me at once.

I hate it. I'd almost rather have the numb cloud of chill I had at the mental hospital. In there, I didn't really care when he told me my mom had died. I understood that I was sad, but it was like I was a hundred miles away from the emotion, like I couldn't reach it.

This is different. This is heart-wrenching. I've never understood what that meant before, but now I know. It feels like your heart is being pulled apart at the seams, and all your feelings are fighting among themselves to be heard.

The police officer clears his throat. "Now, when you called, you said you had escaped from somewhere."

I take another handful of brown paper napkins and blow my nose. "Yes. It was— Well, I thought it was a mental facility."

"What do you mean, like a nuthouse?"

I make a face at the term and wonder if this guy knows how toxic he is. "Like a psychiatric treatment clinic," I clarify. "They told me I had admitted myself, but I think it was all lies. They must have kidnapped me and were keeping me there, because I sure as shit didn't find my way into the woods and check myself in at that place." I swallow and wipe at my wet cheeks, ordering myself not to start in again with the tears.

He looks at my bandaged wrist and holds out his hand. "May I see your wrist?"

I hold it out and he turns it over, then peels back the bandage. "This looks like a suicide attempt," he says sternly, as if I'm in trouble over it.

I yank back my hand. "The woman nurse—she cut my wrist at the clinic. She was going to stage it as a suicide attempt."

He points to the other wrist, where the original cut still had a knotted row of black stitches. "And that one?"

I sighed. "I think they were trying to make me think I had tried to kill myself."

"Right." He lifts his clipboard and goes to write something, then stops. "I'm sorry, I'm confused here. You're saying that a hospital kidnapped you, cut your wrists, and admitted you for treatment?"

"Yeah, I get it. It sounds crazy. It's a fake hospital." I rest my elbows on the table and drop my head into my palms. "The nurse—she's married to the doctor, I think—she's the one who tried to kill me again last night." This is ridiculous. I don't make sense to myself, and I know what I'm saying.

"Tell me your name again?"

"Jessica Bishop. Just go to the place and help the other patients there. I met one on my way out. Her name was Tricia. Tricia Higgins. She said she had kids." As I ran out of the building, I passed so many doors that looked like mine. How many others had someone behind them?

He digests the comment, then continues on. "There's an APB out for you. They've been looking for you. You're aware of what happened to your mom?"

Pentobarbital is what was given to her. You likely put it in her orange juice. You told us that you ordered it online. The more I remember, the more sure I am that I didn't do that. I might not remember how they got me to the clinic, but I remember the days leading up to her death, and I damn sure wasn't planning a murder.

"Yes." I nod. "Well, they told me she was poisoned."

He tilts his head to the side, regarding me, and I can tell he's struggling with what to say. He starts speaking, then pauses. "Miss Bishop . . . do you realize how all of this sounds? You've been missing for six days. You've been a suspect in your mom's death. Now you show up with a story about being in a fake mental institution, with evidence of self-harm—"

"You need to go to the building," I repeat. "Arrest them. The nurse was trying to kill me."

"This is the same nurse who you said attacked the doctor, is that correct?"

I blow out a frustrated breath. "Yes. Just . . . whatever. Arrest me if you want, but go find these people."

He sighs. "Okay. You got a facility name? Address?"

"No. It's like, in the middle of the woods. But close. I can probably find it." I pinch my eyes closed and try to remember how far I drove down the state highway and any landmarks where I entered it. *Head north and use the key fob remote at the gate.* The gate had been hidden from the road, back down a dirt path a ways. I'd have to find the place to turn off. God, why hadn't I paid more attention?

"Well, I've put a call into the detective on your mom's case. Let's get her down here, have her talk to you first."

A woman. That was a good sign. "Okay."

"And you don't know the name of the people who you say were keeping you?"

"The doctor's first name was Joe. I don't remember his last name."

"And the nurse?"

"I think her name was Diana. My mom knew her." I pause. This guy already thinks my story is far-fetched. If I bring up the idea that I might be adopted and that the nurse might be my mom . . . he'll just throw up his hands and ignore the entire thing. Maybe I'll tell the detective that, depending on how she takes the rest of this story. I always thought it'd be cool to be a detective. I think I'd be good at it too.

A car pulls into the parking lot, and I turn at the action. My gaze catches on the Excursion, still parked by the gas station doors, and I straighten. "Oh, that's their car." I point to it. "So can't we just look at the registration?"

His gaze follows to where I'm pointing. "That's their vehicle?"

"Yeah."

He stands up from the table and gestures for me to stay put. "I'll go and look in it. Hey!" He whistles for the second deputy and points to me. "Watch her."

Joke's on him. I found twenty dollars in the center console of the SUV and bought a king-size Reese's Cup and a mega-giant cup of soda. It's the first sugar I've had in a week. I'm in the shade, eating something that isn't a protein shake, and there's a restroom I can use whenever I want to. I wouldn't move from this spot if the building burst into flames.

I watch him walk over to the SUV and wonder how long it will take the detective to get here.

CHAPTER 73

DINAH

Joe's files are in two cabinets in his office at the clinic. It takes me almost ten minutes to transfer them into bankers' boxes and load them into the back seat of the Toyota. I do a final sweep of his office, grabbing our framed wedding photo and his voice recorder, then lock it up. Walking down the hall for a final time, I study each door, thinking of the patients on the other side.

Blythe Howard was never a patient here, but she was our first victim. Joe helped me with it. My therapy sessions turned into planning—all hypothetical at first. He called it an emotional exercise.

The exercise made too much sense, and when I realized that we would never be able to arrest her for the murder of her child, I took the actions we had painstakingly mapped out and killed her.

Afterward, I showed up at Joe's house, emotional and wired, confused at the lack of guilt I felt for such a decisive crime. He brought me in, cooked me dinner, and talked me through every feeling. He told me he was proud of me, and the words were like air in the balloon of my heart.

That night, he kissed me, and it was the sweetest, purest moment of my life.

He quit his job at the LAPD and proposed three months later.

Six months after that, we purchased the land and started construction.

I wanted to put away criminals who were escaping punishment for their crimes. He was fascinated by the possibilities around coercive persuasion and thought control, but unable to conduct proper research with the government's strict limitations on human experimentation.

It was a happy marriage, our two objectives joining forces. And he didn't always kill the patients at the end. Some of the shorter studies were patients pulled from drug-rehab programs and off the streets—those, we nursed back to health and released, and they were none the wiser over the location or true intentions of our facility.

I hesitate at the exit and rest the two heavy boxes of files, mentally tick through the patients we'd be leaving behind. They'll be released, of course. Let back into society with little to no reintroduction therapy or supervision. Would Patient 7 go back to molesting young students? Joe had worked with him for almost two years, had the man repulsed at the thought of any female, old or young—but maybe, back among the public, he'd turn his affections to little boys. Maybe the treatment wouldn't stick. Maybe, maybe, maybe.

I walk out before I have a chance to second-guess the decision. The worst part is that after all this time, all this hard work, this place will never get the recognition it deserves. Joe will never get the recognition he deserves. Instead, they will paint this place as hell, with all the focus going to the process and not the results.

It will be easier in Costa Rica. Their laws are much more lenient—practically nonexistent—on psychiatric testing. Individuals can volunteer for paid trials, which means that with enough money, anything is possible.

I'm backing out when one of the two cell phones in my pocket rings. Putting the SUV into park, I dig out the offending phone. It's mine, and the first six numbers of the incoming call indicates someone in the LAPD. I silence it and start the engine, then double-check the gas level.

It's full, as are the tires and all the fluids. Joe has the vehicle serviced regularly, and in the back is an emergency blanket, a case of bottled water, and a first aid kit. I used to make fun of him for his excessive prep measures. Under the back seat are supplies of a different tilt: duct tape, zip ties, gloves, tarps, ponchos, and booties. This vehicle is one we bought from a surplus auction using cash. It's titled under a shell corporation that would take weeks to link back to us. It doesn't have GPS or toll meters, which is why it has a glass jar full of quarters in the center console.

The missed caller leaves a voicemail and I play it, steeling myself for Natalie's voice. In all this excitement, I haven't had a chance to go through my phone since I got it back. Given this new twist, I'm not sure it makes sense to. We'll need to ditch both of our phones, anyway, as soon as we hit the main road. In the suitcases are burners, purchased years ago specifically for this purpose.

Preparation, Joe has always preached, is the key to success.

The voicemail isn't from Natalie. It's from an officer I've never met. Chuck Reynolds. He has a potential eyewitness and suspect in the current case for Reese Bishop—her missing daughter, Jessica. He won't shut up in his voicemail, giving me his current location and a bit about what the girl is saying. He finishes by asking me to call him as soon as possible.

So, she made it out. I place the phone in the cup holder and sit back, thinking.

It's ironic that they contacted me. Later, they'll laugh about it. Reynolds will get a ration of shit for calling the kidnapper and telling her where her escaped victim is. I can't go get her, though the idea of taking her back and us resuming our clinic protocols is a little tempting, if not completely unrealistic.

Still, I hate the thought of running away and leaving our house that we put so much time and love into. Never coming back to all our favorite places and the memories of each one. Joe's job at the college. Oley's grave. I'll lose my detective's shield, which I worked so hard for. Joe's medical degree. My mom's constant calls and check-ins. Except for the summer when I had Jessica, I've never gone more than a couple of days without speaking to her. The silence of that summer was hell. Hell with a labor-inducing cherry on top.

I delete the voicemail and shift the SUV into reverse. After carefully backing out, I head toward the house to collect my husband.

CHAPTER 74

JESSICA

I haven't been home yet, but they keep promising that they'll let me go soon. I don't seem to be a suspect in my mom's death, which is good, I guess. I'm still crying at random moments, and I keep expecting to run out of tears, but it doesn't seem like it's going to happen.

I asked the officer if he knew where my phone was, and he gave me a blank look, then said that I'll probably need to get a new one. I don't want to nag him about it, but I still have like twenty-one payments left on it, and I didn't get insurance.

Now I'm in a holding room. A cute officer brought me some food. He was really tall, like a basketball player. I asked if he wanted some of my fries, and he turned me down, but he smiled when he said it. He sat down at the table and talked to me while I ate. Even brought me a cup of ice.

Mom would have liked him. She always had a weakness for tall guys. *Give me a loser*, she once said, *as long as he's tall.*

He left after a few minutes, and I've been alone since, just sitting in this room like I'm in time-out. You'd think they'd have some magazines or something in here. It's just a table and two chairs. Not even a wastebasket for my trash.

The door to the room opens, and I put down the fry I am about to eat. A woman in a suit walks in, all business and a big smile, and maybe she's the detective.

"Hi, Jessica." Her bright-red lipstick is a little too orange, and her mascara is caked on, but her eyes seem nice. Mom always said you could tell a lot about a person through their eyes, which seemed valid except that Dr. Joe had eyes a cat would curl up in and was likely a killer psychopath. "My name is Natalie Force. I'm the chief of police for the LAPD."

I stand up and shake the hand she offers. I'd never met a chief of police before, but she doesn't look like what I imagined. "Hi."

"I know you've already given a statement, but I had a few questions for you, if you don't mind repeating some of it again."

"I'm not crazy." I sit back down and pull my fries closer to me. "I know my story sounds like it, but—"

"I don't think you're crazy. I think your statement is accurate." She takes the other seat and links her fingers together on top of the table.

"You do?"

"I just came from the clinic where you were kept. We were able to get inside, and there were four other women being kept there. They all have stories very similar to yours, at least in terms of the operation of the . . . ah, facility." She pauses and stares into my eyes. "Jessica, some of these women—we've been looking for them for years."

Four other women. *Years.* I was in knots after just a week; how did they make it that long? I eat another fry, then start to gather my trash and return it to the bag.

Four women. Were they all here, each in little private rooms, waiting to share their story while they wolf down their own double cheeseburgers and fries?

"There are some interesting parallels between the detective working your mother's case and the woman you described as the nurse." She withdraws a phone and taps the screen, then holds it up, showing me an image. "Is this the woman who was your nurse?"

It's her in a police uniform, cap under one arm. She's smiling, and I flinch because her smile looks just like mine. Kinda slanted on the side, like our heart isn't in it. Another thing Mom used to say. Did she realize the similarities in our smile?

"Yeah." The word croaks out and I swallow, then try again. "That's her."

"This is Dinah Marino. She's not a nurse, but she is married to a clinical psychologist, Dr. Joe Marino. I've been trying to track down Dinah ever since yesterday, when she missed an important appointment."

So they *are* married. And she's a police officer. I stare at the photo. "What's the connection between her and the detective assigned to my mom's case?"

"She is the detective assigned to your mother's case. We're trying to understand the history now. Can you tell me when and how you were taken?"

She's the detective assigned to your mother's case. The thought makes my head spin. I think of the file Dr. Joe showed me, one he must have gotten from her. To think that she was investigating my mom's murder while her husband was telling me that I did it . . . I frown. "I don't know how I was taken. I woke up in the hospital room."

"The room at the clinic?"

"Yes."

"Was this the day your mother passed?"

"I don't know. The last memory I have is going to bed Monday night. I watched some TV in bed and went to sleep. What . . . when was she found?"

"Thursday afternoon. The mail carrier saw her through the window."

Poor Henry. He fed Bunny when we went to Washington for the week. When Bunny died, he dug a hole in the side yard for us to put her body in.

I push back the memory and make a note to both thank and apologize to the mailman the next time I see him. Mom used to make him her chocolate chip cookies. Tears spring at the thought that she would never again make them. That had been on my list of things to learn from her before she was gone. Chocolate chip cookies. Her veal parmigiana. The breakfast-burrito tacos. Maybe there were some recipe cards in the kitchen somewhere.

"Do you have any questions for me, Jessica?" the woman asks.

"Did you arrest them?"

She immediately shakes her head. "No. We're looking for both of them now. Don't worry, we'll make sure you're safe. As soon as you're done here, I'll have an officer escort you home, and we'll keep a car at your house until they are in custody."

"You think they'll come to get me?"

She smiles again, and I think she means it to be reassuring but it's not. "No. It looks like they're on the run. Likely to Mexico. We found a vehicle they had registered under a shell corporation and are looking for it now. We've got a flag on their IDs and all of their credit cards and accounts, so we'll find them in the next few hours. They will have to stop for gas or will go to an airport, or will get on a bus or cross at the border—and we'll get them. It's not a question of *if*, just *when*. But the last thing they're thinking about right now is you. They're looking to escape."

"I didn't kill my mom." It seems strange that no one has asked me that question yet, when it seemed to be all Dr. Joe cared about.

"We don't think you killed your mom." She smiles at me again, and even though I like everything this woman is saying, I don't like her.

CHAPTER 75

DINAH

One week later

"Three letters. Flightless bird." I say the clue out loud for his benefit as I write it in: E-M-U.

Joe takes a bite of his sandwich as he eyes the puzzle. We are side by side in the booth, our shoulders touching, elbows brushing as we eat. I am on the right side so I can write without poking him, and every once in a while, his knee bumps against mine underneath the table.

Each touch gives me a jolt of giddiness. When my mom told me our spark would die after a few months of marriage, she'd never been so wrong.

"Want my fries?" I ask, noticing that he's eaten all his.

"No." He picks up his tea and rattles the ice, then takes a sip.

I try not to react at the lack of a *thank you* at the end of his response. It's punishment. He's making it as clear as he can that he is still mad at me. It's fine; I didn't expect instant forgiveness. After all, I've uprooted our entire life.

He's of the staunch opinion I should have let him kill Jessica in the house. If I had, we wouldn't be road-tripping through Central America, our entire life left back in California. He doesn't understand why I stopped him, and I don't understand why it doesn't occur to him that a mother—even an estranged mother who never had a relationship with her daughter—might not want to see that daughter killed.

Yes, I was about to kill her myself, but would I have gone through with it? Maybe I wouldn't have. A week out from the event, I'm thinking that I had hesitated. That my motherly instincts were starting to kick in and that I would have set down the scalpel and walked away.

And yes, I am responsible for us uprooting our lives, but I had a reason to be mad at him also. He was brushing all his actions to the side, diminishing them in the light of my exposed secrets, but I haven't forgotten everything he has said or done to me.

A black SUV pulls into the parking lot and parks beside a big dusty bus. I watch it as I take a bite of a chicken tender with too much breading. So far, the food sucks, but maybe that's what we get, ordering like a bunch of Americans. I'll reserve judgment until after we are settled in Costa Rica and have a chance to sample all local cuisines.

"Forty-six down is *befuddled.*" Joe chews, then wipes the corner of his mouth with a brown paper napkin.

I move my pen to the spot without checking the clue and write it in. Trust in your partner is crucial, which is why I understand that my deceit is hard for him to overcome or forgive. It will take time, but that's okay because we have lots of it now. No cases on my end. No patients or students on his. Nothing but the empty road and three more stops before Costa Rica. I reach over and touch his hand. He pulls it away and I sigh, then look back at the crossword.

"Mr. and Mrs. Marino?"

There is an officer standing at the table, and I look away from him and out the window, and that's when I see a row of local police cars, all parked at various angles, their noses pointing toward the restaurant. On the edge, there's a black SUV, two suits standing beside it, and I bet my platter of chicken tenders that they are Feds.

It's a scene I've been in a number of times, only in those incidents, I was the one in the uniform, on the periphery, watching as the Feds swooped in on a guilty target.

I wait for the panic to swell, my body to stiffen, my fight-or-flight instincts to flare to life, but instead I feel a deflation of everything in my soul.

It is over. We are not going to *Thelma & Louise* our way out of this. Death is not worth the escape, and Joe and I are not built for combat. We fight with our brains, not our brawn, and this scenario is on our extension escape plan.

If cornered, if caught, surrender. Let the lawyers and the loopholes get us out. Don't confess to anything. Don't say anything. Keep your mouth shut, and let our money work.

"Joe." I nudge my husband with my elbow, pulling his attention away from the officer and to the view out the window. "Look."

And just that quickly, our run comes to an end. I reach over and grab hold of his hand, and this time, he doesn't pull it away. He turns his palm over and squeezes, and our eyes meet across the table, and it's just like the first time I met him, in his office, on the ninth floor of the west-department tower. That solid, reassuring, warm look that told me everything was going to be all right.

CHAPTER 76

JESSICA

Every day of their trial, I sit in the back room of the courthouse and watch. I am still trying to figure out how I feel about Dinah. I hate her for what she did. That was a hard day, the day they went through her testimony on the night she kidnapped me and put out the poison for Mom.

Mom always took her pills. She approached fighting heart disease like she would a job, and doing a good job at work was like, number one on her list of shit that is important. She also always fixed coffee before work. Apparently, when she met Dinah for lunch, she raved about her morning coffee routine, which is how Dinah knew that the vanilla-hazelnut creamer would be used.

Even though I hate Dinah, I also feel sorry for her. Her mom testified on her behalf. Said a lot of really nice things about her. So did her sister, who is apparently married to my dad.

I know. This is like *E! True Hollywood Story* shit. Netflix literally sent someone to the house and offered me half a million dollars for the film rights to it. They said they had a major A-list actress who had already agreed to play me in it and everything.

I signed their offer. Drove that check right down to the bank and deposited it, and used the money to pay off Mom's mortgage. Now at least I don't have to worry about that each month, though I hate sleeping in the house where all this bad stuff happened.

My dad—that sounds SO weird to say—showed up at Chunky Mike's one day and introduced himself. He seems like an okay guy, even if he did bang two sisters. He stared at me a lot; maybe he was trying to see himself in me. He showed me pictures of his daughters, who I guess are my . . . let's see, we were trying to figure this out after he left. They are my half sisters *and* also my cousins.

Cue the banjo music, right? He seems just as weirded out by it as I am, and when I told him it was okay, that I didn't need to have a relationship with him, he was *super* relieved. Like, offensively so. I mean, he could have at least been like, "Oh, are you sure? I'd love to get to know you," or something, but nope. He practically skipped out the door; the only reason he didn't was because he wanted Magic Shell on his cone, which is like the single biggest pain-in-the-ass order for us to do, by the way.

Zach—he's my new boyfriend—thinks that the jury is going to deem Dinah and Joe insane and put them in a long-term-care crazy house. Which is like, so ironic, but also kind of bullshit. That woman I saw on my way out of the facility, her name is Tricia Higgins, and she said they kept her there for three years and tried to convince her that she was addicted to nicotine and had lost a husband in a drowning accident. She's not even married, but she said she believed it, all the way up until they released her and told her it wasn't true.

Zach is moving in with me next week. He says I need protection, which I agree, and I am beyond excited about having my first real adult relationship. He's so much more mature than the other guys I've dated, and he's like, obsessed with me. And Mom would be thrilled to know that he's an assistant manager at an extermination company, which isn't exactly a doctor but it's a good five steps above every noncommittal loser I've dated in the past.

I really do hope Mom would like him. And also that she'd be okay with us moving in together, especially since it's her house. I also wonder if she'd be cool if I visited Dinah at some point, once she goes off to prison. I mean, she had wanted us to have a relationship. I think that's why she first told me about her, once she found out she was dying. Inventing an estranged sister was an odd way to go about it, but maybe she thought that was a baby step to confessing that I am adopted. I don't know but it's weird now, not having a mom. I didn't realize how much I depended on her for everything. And I definitely didn't give her credit for how smart she was. Like, looking back, all the advice she ever gave me was right. Except the whole *you should date a doctor* thing. I mean, Dinah did that, and look what happened to her.

Anyway, Mom, if you're listening, I love you and miss you, and that ficus plant that you always said I was gonna kill—it's still alive. Just like me. We're fighters, just like you were. Just like you'll always be in my mind.

Thank you for adopting me. You were the best thing that ever happened in my life.

Epilogue

DINAH

One year later

"Let me know if you see any that look like railroad tracks." I lean over the table, scanning the sea of puzzle pieces.

"Okay." Joe doesn't look up, his focus on a handful of edge pieces that he's assembling.

I spot one and then another, and add them to my pile, then stand up and stretch my back. "I'm going to grab a coffee. Want one?"

He nods and our eyes meet for a moment, and he gives me a small smile. My heart soars, and I return the expression. As I pass his chair, I squeeze his shoulder. He's been working out, and I can feel the difference. I like the changes that two hours a day in the gym brings to my husband. His arms are more defined, his biceps stretching out the sleeves of his shirt. His face has thinned out a little, his jaw more defined as a result.

I didn't think it was possible, but my husband is even hotter than before. Not as tan, true, but still deliciously sexy. I've heard the whispers among the staff, seen the lingering looks the female patients give him. Everyone wants him, but I am the only one who has his heart.

Even with everything I did, it's still mine. We spent a year apart, in separate jails, awaiting our trials and sentencing. It was the hardest year of my life, time we passed with letters sent via post office. It was actually quite romantic, our courtship by mail. I wrote him a letter every day, in the hour before I went to bed. He did the same, sending me more than three hundred letters. I kept every single one of them, storing them in a box that is now under my bed, ready to pull out if I ever need a moment of reassurance.

In that year, in those letters, we healed and strengthened every weak point and break that the prior decade created between us. By the time we left the jail, we were as strong as iron and ready to tackle the next chapter of our life. A chapter that, thanks to our unlimited budget for legal fees, will be in comfort. Our new home doesn't have the character of our old one, but it allows us to spend every day together, which is what we wanted.

I grab two cups from the rack and smile at the attendant. I fill both our cups with light roast and fix his first, adding a splash of almond milk and one Stevia packet. As I slip a java sleeve on the cup, I watch Joe working, his brow wrinkled in concentration as he hunches over the pieces.

We will spend the next three decades in this facility. After that, we are up for appeal, though our attorney has made it clear that we shouldn't count on a release. That's fine with me. My biggest fear would be that one of us would be released and not the other. Together, we can be happy. It's not the most exciting existence, but we're finding our own entertainment in the walls of this place.

I stir my coffee and look over the schedule tacked to the mental facility's bulletin board. Today is Tuesday, and I find the menu and review the choices. Chicken alfredo with minestrone soup. I glance at the clock on the wall. Still two hours before lunch begins. We normally take ours outside on the deck that overlooks the gardens. I'll spend the afternoon in those gardens while Joe will hit the gym. Tonight, we'll have a light supper, then play Ping-Pong in the rec center before retiring to bed.

We have separate rooms, but we're used to sleeping in our own beds. At least we aren't judged for it here. I pick up his coffee and return to our table, ignoring the wave from a patient whom I pass. We haven't made many friends here; Joe and I are unique. I don't want to say that we're better than the rest, but we are here by choice, not necessity. This place is a carnival of medical conditions, everything from addictions to PTSD to dissociative disorders. Not the genetic makeup that I want in a new friend group.

I took my family off the approved visitor's list, and the act was similar to removing an anchor. I had become too dependent on them, and it took leaving that cocoon to realize how stifling it was. Now I can breathe. And I don't miss them. Especially not Marci. This situation finally gives me the excuse to break off our relationship—an excuse I've wanted for twenty-two years. Finally, no more of her and him. Every time I saw him touch her, beam at her, kiss her . . . it was a fresh knife stabbing into my heart. Not that I ever loved him, but for that entire summer when I was away, our baby growing bigger in my stomach, I loved the idea of him. I envisioned us raising our child together, of going public with our relationship, of having him get down on one knee and beam at me and ask me to be his wife.

Instead, I returned from that summer with stretch marks and a second chin to find his arm around her waist, a hickey on her neck. When he got her pregnant the summer after her high school graduation, she wasn't shipped away. No, instead they married, and my first love became my brother-in-law. A near-constant reminder of the life that didn't happen. The baby who was given away. The betrayal of my sister and the rejection of my crush.

He had taken my virginity by the trash cans outside our house. That's where he'd pulled me, when we realized that my dad was asleep on the couch and Marci was up in my bedroom. He had a few beers tucked in his pockets, and we leaned against the house and I chugged them, desperate for his approval, and when he kissed me, I clung to him, and when he unbuttoned my pants, I let him.

It wasn't forced or with a stranger, despite what I told Joe in that joint session with Jessica. It was sloppy and painful, but quick—less than a minute from entrance to exit. He had grinned at me afterward, as if he'd given me something special. And he had, we just didn't realize it then. He didn't realize it until twenty-one years later, when it was revealed during the trial.

I didn't have to share Jessica's paternity during my testimony, but I did. In part because Marci was in the front row, her hand possessively on his thigh, despite my repeated requests for them not to attend the trial.

It was my parting punch to them, a punch that hit Marci in the gut, her eyes going wide, her face white. She looked like she was going to faint, then vomit, and I recognized that reaction. Now she knew, at least on a small scale, what betrayal felt like.

I confessed the truth of the paternity in that evening's love letter to Joe. It's amazing how easy it is to be transparent and honest when you don't have to deliver the news in person.

His response was kind and forgiving, and I'm sure it helped that he had a day to digest the information before he penned a reaction. That, and the fact that I was already broken in his mind. This confession was just one more crack. One more thing on a future list of items to fix.

My husband loves a project, and while I am no longer supplying him with emotionally damaged and guilty patients to experiment on, he has a newer, better project: his wife. Oh, he's being crafty with his therapy. He is nibbling at one piece of trauma at a time, savoring and enjoying that chunk before moving on to the next.

When he exhausts my well of deceit, when I have no other cracked pieces to mend, then I'll find him a new project. An easy task in a facility for the criminally insane. But for now, I'm keeping him busy, and I love having his full and undivided attention.

I place the coffee in front of my husband and retake my seat.

"Thanks." He picks up his cup and watches as I do the same. Holding it out, he clinks it to mine. "To the love of my life," he says. "Forever and always."

"Forever and always," I repeat, and meet my husband's eyes.

Till death do us part.

—Dinah Marino, Patient #423, Walworth Institute,
private medical facility

Acknowledgments

While I will try not to get emotional during the writing of these acknowledgments, I must confess that there's a bit of a feelings dump that occurs during the final days of a book's editorial life. This is the last step in the process and similar to the final, bittersweet sweep through a house once the movers have cleared everything out. As I took my final read, I tried to enjoy the story through a reader's eyes. It's an almost impossible task, as my brain is too busy trying to gauge if the scenes hit right, if the characters feel authentic, if the dark moments are too dark, the pacing too quick, the climax too short . . . you get the drift.

My security blanket, as I furiously flipped through the pages, was the knowledge that my overly critical eyes were not alone. I've been blessed to have a bevy of brilliant creatives beside me on every step of this book's journey.

I am not exaggerating or boastful when I say that the best in the business have worked on this novel, and I am so grateful to each one of them—for their unwavering patience, creative insights, tireless dedication, and wealth of experience.

This book, dear reader, was such a wild and fun ride to create—and I'd like to take a moment to thank a few of the many people who made it possible. First off, my ride-or-die agent, Maura Kye-Casella, who keeps me laughing, could definitely protect me in a dark alley, and is always available whenever I need advice, a brainstorm partner, or an NYC travel recommendation. I am continually grateful that our paths crossed thirteen years ago, back when I was a newbie author with one book to my name. Secondly, the great and brilliant Megha Parekh, who has been championing and believing in me for years before we had the pleasure to work together. You are a saint for navigating my ever-changing plot twists and character whims. Thank you for your patience and faith, even when the story takes detours we never planned for. Your ideas and encouragement are invaluable, and I'm forever grateful to have you in my corner. Thank you for all the phone calls, the deadline extensions, your support, and your keen insights.

To the incredible Charlotte Herscher, who is such a master of developmental editing. You have a fantastic ability to see potentials in my (very, very) rough draft and the steps to carve it into shape. Your edits continually improve my craft and elevate my stories in such a powerful way. I can't wait to do a dozen more together.

To Rachel Norfleet, my meticulous copyeditor, and your team. You are all saints for navigating my comma usage, invented words, and questionable timelines. Thank you for the fact-checking, error corrections, continuity catches, and more. A special shout-out of appreciation to Andrea Nauta, Sarah Vostok, and Jessica Poore. I'm endlessly grateful for your expertise.

Thank you to the entire Thomas & Mercer team. Gracie, Darci, Heather, Jarrod, and everyone behind the scenes—your passion and dedication help my books find their way into readers' hands and allow me to spend time where I am happiest, in the writing cave. I'm endlessly appreciative of all that you do.

To my family, who remain the bedrock of my world: Your love and support sustain me, even through the late nights, the messy drafts, and the "just one more chapter" writing binges. Whiskey, I miss you more than anything and will always remember you being by my side during the late-night writing sessions, guarding my office door.

And finally, to you—my readers. Thank you for choosing to spend your time with my words, for supporting each new story, and for sticking with me through every twist and turn. I hope that reading it brought you even a fraction of the joy that creating it brought me. If you'd like to stay connected or learn about what I'm working on next, you can find me on TikTok, IG, and at www.alessandratorre.com/newsletter.

With gratitude,
Alessandra (A. R.) Torre

About the Author

Photo © 2022 Jane Ashley Converse

A. R. Torre is a pseudonym for *New York Times* bestselling author Alessandra Torre. She has been featured in such publications as *ELLE* and *ELLE* UK and has guest-blogged for *Cosmopolitan* and the *Huffington Post*. In addition, Torre is the co-creator of Inkers Con, a community and events coordinator for authors. For more information about Alessandra, visit www.alessandratorre.com.